MY GOAT ATE ITS OWN LEGS

MY GOAT ATE ITS OWN LEGS | ALEX BURRETT

30 TALES OF VARYING LENGTHS FOR ADULTS

Burninghouse

First published 2008.

A Burning House book.

www.burninghousebooks.com

Burning House is an imprint of
Beautiful Books Limited
36-38 Glasshouse Street
London W1B 5DL

ISBN 9781905636372

9 8 7 6 5 4 3 2 1

A catalogue reference for this book is available from the British Library.

Cover design by Studio Dempsey.
Typeset by Ellipsis Books Limited, Glasgow.
Printed in Great Britain by CPI Mackays, Chatham ME5 8TD

For Morgan, Lauren and Gorse

CONTENTS

MY GOAT ATE ITS OWN LEGS

My goat ate its own legs. I'd left it in the field on its own for a month. It was the first holiday I'd had for eight years. Farm animals happily graze uninterfered with during the summer. In fact, many prefer to be left alone. And goats are the hardiest of all the domesticated species. There was plenty of grass. And water. A stream runs through the wandering channel it has cut through the soft earth of my goat's fertile pasture. I presumed it would be fine. How was I to know that a plague of locusts would strike a couple of days into my break – eating every sprouting plant and herbaceous thing?

Before it ate its own legs, my goat ate: the blankets in the barn; two saddles; an old tractor tyre; the bark off the huge tree in the bottom corner of the field; and the number plate and light covers off the trailer backed-up near the top end. It always had a healthy appetite. When I returned home, I thought it was as gone as the grass and other organic material. My first scan of a once-healthy field revealed a goatless post-nuclear wasteland. The rich variety of greens had been replaced with a singular, homogenous, oppressive brown. Everything blended into one – the scorched earth, the stripped-down bare wooden shed, the pared trunk. As I stared in disbelief and dejection, I noticed a feature – my goat's head. It was jutting up from the stream's sodden furrow like a seal's inquisitive domed crown poking above a rolling coastal wave. Spirits instantly raised, I vaulted the barrier-gate like an ancient Olympian, and rocketed towards it. I cared nothing for the grass, or the tree, or anything else on my farm that was lost. I loved my goat. Charging gleefully across the field, homing in on its friendly face like a flesh-coloured cruise missile locked on target, I imagined it lying beside the stream, tired and hungry but complete. I didn't imagine it was lying there legless. It was.

My goat lives on the pond now. It grazes on the lush grasses that thrive on the watery banks. The vet advised putting it down, but that goat has been my best friend for years. I've built a raft around it with a tightly secured harness that holds its limbless body in place and upright. A system of criss-cross and herringbone straps fixed over its back and shoulders ensures it never overturns. Goes tits-up. The goat's back end droops into the water. To propel itself around it shakes its arse. It's become incredibly adept at manoeuvring, and can even reverse by performing strange circular tail wags. Some say it's cruel, but my goat has been happily strapped to that raft, voyaging around the pond for the past two years. On particularly cold days, I land it in a dry dock I've built near my farmhouse. There I feed it on thick oats and moist sugar beet – that's a pretty luxurious diet for a farm animal. And yet it always yearns to get back into the water. My uncle believes that's because it's in control of its own destiny on the pond. It has the freedom of choosing where to go and where to graze. I disagree. I'm sure it's that when it's in the water, all four stumps hidden under the surface, it can kick them and imagine it's got four legs again, and that we're prancing round the old field like we used to, chasing each other.

THE STONE

During childhood, one of my best friends was a stone. It never changed or moved. I always knew where to find it. Right now, as you're reading this, I imagine it's exactly where it always was. Unchanged. It's a pretty big stone; it's longer than a seven-year-old head to toe, but shorter than a twelve-year-old head-to-toe. I think it's limestone; one of the denser, harder varieties. When I think of its immutable form, it feels like it should be granite, but I don't think there is any granite in that area. And granite is too tough, too cold. My stone has more life about it.

Limestone is the modelling clay of rock types. It can be moulded into innumerable wonderful designs; designs devoid of the hard corners and severe faces of other stones. Limestone is borne of life. It is comprised from the compressed shells of living creatures. Once mature, it's slowly mutating guises are shaped by passionate swirling water and tempestuous falling rain. This epochal process outlives the evolution, and extinction, of entire species. Limestone is organic in every sense. My stone is no exception. It's flattish. Guessing how tall I was at various stages of my relationship with it, I'd say the stone is about a metre long. It's probably an average of forty centimetres wide and about twenty centimetres deep, but, being a natural object, the length, width and depth vary at any two points of measurement. No word can define its shape.

If we had a word for every shape imaginable, there would be no room in our vocabularies for love or hate. The closest way to describe the shape of my stone would be to call it rectangular or oblong. But those words are oppressively geometric, and hence hugely misleading. The stone is shaped like a bow-tie that has been tied really badly, with a really fat loose knot, so that it doesn't corset much in the middle; then ironed super-flat so the constriction in the middle is even less defined; then twisted and pulled in every direction; then ironed all over again; then mauled; then ironed countless times until its shape is indescribable; then attached to a cat's collar for a week of prowling through undergrowth. More specifically, one end of the stone is narrower than the other. At a few points it is quite deep. Here and there it is thinner – both near the edges, and also at some points between the edges. And yet its form is only half of what makes it so special. Equally important is its situation. It lies, face down, in the middle of a young, gurgling stream. It lies there, regardless of time or weather, unflinchingly dependable. These two factors combine in Gestalt fashion to create a wonderful object. Being the shape it is, and lying where it does, means that it offers several perfect places for trapping trout.

I used to catch trout with my hands. I lived in a rural area. There were no kids to play ball games with. The bubbling brook was my chattering clique. You may have heard of tickling trout. For the record, I lived amongst trout for a dozen years and I've no idea how you would get close enough to a trout to tickle it. If a trout glimpses your silhouette or moving shadow, it becomes an underwater rabbit racing for its burrow. It darts for cover, its streamline brown fleshy form the underwater blur of a living torpedo. Once in shelter, it'll stay in its hiding place for far longer

4

than a young boy is willing to wait for it to emerge. The advantage we have over these slippery sprinters is intelligence – we're not at the top of the food chain for nothing. Trout are creatures of instinct. Back then, I interpreted that as habit. They have favourite hiding spots. Some will head for a clump of water weed, some cower under overhanging turf, some disappear under large rocks lying in the water. Most rocks offer only one hiding place. Larger ones like my stone, can provide several. I knew the rocks of that gluggling brook as well as I know the faces of my children. I knew their every curve and point and dimple. I knew them, as if I'd studied them from the day they broke free from the bedrock, through every shaping force, to the moment they came to rest in my stream. My long flattish stone, I knew best of all. There were six trout hiding places under my stone. Three of these were smaller pockets at the edges. Two were larger, with more features – nooks and crannies that needed gentle, knowledgeable finger-exploration. The sixth hole was the mother of all trout hides – it was an underwater tunnel emerging at two opposite points near the narrower end of the stone. The trout loved that tunnel. In my early fishing days, I hated it.

Every time I went trout-hunting in that stream, I could feel the gravitation pull of my trusty stone. Even if I set out to fish another section of the water, inevitably it would draw me to it. One minute I'd be wandering through the musty wood upstream, or duelling with herons downstream, the next I'd be back in the same old spot, kicking up a frantic froth, herding trout underneath that steadfast boulder. The approach routine was as practised as the Changing of the Guard. I'd lie down on the stone's cold, water-splattered surface. My clothes would instantly soak up clear fresh water. I'd smell the wet rock up-close; a base note of wet stone, sprinkled with the watered-down vegetative smell of desperate lichen and displaced sediment. As I lay there half-drenched, I'd convince myself I was truly free, that I'd escaped the predictable ways of the human world to interact instinctively with the natural one. My hands would break the water's surface. Anxious, agitated fingers, chilled to the bone, would move around underneath, investigating all the lesser holes and trout hides. But my fantasy of having thrown off the shackles of conformity was a delusion, because from the moment my fingertips pierced the water's surface, my mind would be elsewhere. Even my hands anticipated the main event. I fished that stone like a guardsman giving a royal salute with his rifle – my performance was formulaic and the outcome was inevitable.

Excepting the tunnel, the holes under that rock were easy. I knew how to move into all of them, covering escape routes with my arms; contorting my palms into fleshy vices; prodding with numb, knuckle-grated fingers. But trying to enjoy those holes was like expecting satisfaction from beating a toddler at football – because the biggest trout in the brook loved the tunnel. It was big, it was dark and to them it seemed entirely safe. Their faith in that haven annoyed me, so, soon after arriving at the rock, I'd find myself abandoning the lesser five dens, desperately trying to grasp a prize trout by thrusting a hand down one end of the long tunnel – only to see a vision of piscine beauty zoom silently out of the other.

Logically the tunnel was the opposite of the safe harbour that trout believed it to be. It was a perfect natural fish trap. That knowledge drew little me to it. I grew bigger. The stone stayed the same size. Finally, one year, when the weather was once again warm enough to bear two hours standing and kneeling in chilled

6

spring water, I lay on the familiar stone and something had changed. My shoulders were wide enough, and my arms long enough, to allow my hands to meet in the middle of the tunnel. The game was up for the big fish.

Catching the best trout in the stream became as easy as putting on a pair of gloves. The struggle for mastery of the master tunnel was over. No scaly underwater rocket could escape my grasp. They were ensnared. One hand would drive them while the other hand was the ready net. My enthusiasm for catching trout with my hands started to wane around that time. I don't know whether I'd reached an age where other things – like girls – became more interesting, or that the mastering of this once-useless trout trap turned an erstwhile sport into a predictable event. Whatever the reason, my passion for *poisson* evaporated before that Autumn's fruits were ripe and juicy. I changed. In fact, everything changed during my years living near that stream. I grew bigger, altered shape. The structure of my family home, constructed from chunks of the same rock, transformed. I lost my youthful naivety – and my virginity. I left school. My parents split up. I left home. They sold the house. New people moved in and the new people changed the house even further. In total, over twenty years have passed since I regularly baited the trout of that brook. In that time, I've become cynical and less agile. Falling over hurts more. I put on weight all too easily now. Lines scar my face. I cry for different reasons. The stone won't have changed. It's still a big chunk of useless limestone lying in a scarcely visited strip of water.

That stone serves two purposes. It's a shelter for nervous trout, and it's an anchor connecting me to my past. It's an anchor because it's the only unchanged thing from my childhood. Throughout all the trauma of growing-up and getting hurt, it was resolutely fixed. It was, forever dependably, a fairly big, fairly flat, irregularly-shaped chunk of limestone, lying on its belly in a meandering stream. It was always in the same place. It was always there for me. When I think of my life, and become disturbed by all the things that have gone wrong, I journey there in my mind. I close my eyes, shutting out the endlessly shifting world, and I'm a young, motivated, purposeful, short-wearing lad again. Climbing over barbed-wire fences, making my way through unkempt copses, heading for that stone. Then I'm lying on it, plunging my little hands into cold running water, feeling for trout.

DATING DEATH

A friend of mine dated Death. It was never going to last forever, I could see that from the start. They had a certain chemistry, but the potion was wrong. They were oil and vinegar. For a while they were truly great together, but their eventual separation was inevitable. Anybody who knew them both as well as I did would have predicted the same fate. With the preconceptions most people have about Death, you might think that whatever went wrong was his fault. But the break-up wasn't just down to him. Fair enough, he does deserve some of his infamous reputation – but she's no angel.

They first met when she stabbed herself in the heart with an electrified kebab skewer. She'd had her heart broken and wanted to physically rupture it, stop it dead, in response. He admired the poetry of her unique suicide attempt. He was also impressed by her technical ability to build an elaborate death device using household materials. And he admired her no-nonsense, unegotistical spirit. She hadn't once talked about death or suicide before her attempt on her life. And she didn't regard it as some kind of tragic, glorious gesture. She just got dumped on by a total dickhead and decided to fry her own heart in response. The decision was that easy. For her, deciding to force a mains-connected spike between two ribs and drive it home into her healthy blood-pump, was like deciding to open a bottle of wine, or toast a slice of bread. She approached her self-destructive task with discipline and accuracy. Her weapon was faultless. Once constructed, handling her home-made mortifier required great care and scientific understanding – she needed to maintain a highly sophisticated grasp of physics and biology to operate it. An impending one-way trip into the hereafter didn't intimidate her into making a mistake. Death told me that, generally, even the brightest sparks, when engaged in the process of taking their own lives, are transformed into clumsy idiots, drunk with mental anguish. She was different. She managed to stay completely composed while driven by the insane urge to take her own life. Throughout her preparations for self-annihilation, she never once lost her dignity. She didn't crack-up. She didn't degrade herself by falling into decline. She didn't let her high standards of personal presentation slip. She didn't make a mess of her home or her body. Even the puncture point in her breast was neat and accurately chosen. In summary, she executed her plan with the professionalism and clinical accuracy of a surgeon – which is what she is – and it worked almost perfectly (she survived). Death admired that level of resolve – he told me it was practically unheard of. My friend is dauntingly intelligent, stunningly beautiful and wildly passionate, but on top of all this, she's utterly unfazed by the prospect of death. Death rates that quality of hers above all others. He told me that amongst the expiring hoards, there are just a handful of women like her every millennia – and he's seen them all. Well, all the dead ones at least – which accounts for most humans who've ever lived. Let's face it, no regular Jo is going to pull Death.

Death and I were chatting at a house party once (we often found one another hanging out near the knives in the kitchen) and he described some of the myriad women who've thrown themselves at him. He's had every type of female make moves on him; young, old, religious, faithless, stunning, grotesque, stupid, brilliant. The ones he dislikes most of all, are the ones that worship him; dedicate themselves to him. The hardest type to find are those who are indifferent to his charms. My friend was indifferent to death to the extreme. Wilful, fearless and interesting people like her are the ones Death really respects.

We're all going to die Death loves to remind me. So why do we obsess with the one event that is utterly predictable? Death has never understood why, if we truly value life, so many of us spend much of it obsessing about him. He'll meet us all one day and since that's an undeniable fact, he can't comprehend why we constantly squander time trying to guess what he's like. We all get it wrong anyway. He describes the act of death as being like a present, wrapped-up, in the corner of a room. Some of us will feel and shake it, trying to guess what it is. Some will peel back bits of paper to try to get a peek at what's inside. Others just won't leave it alone until they discover for themselves what it is. He says an obsession with what's in the box is a mark of an immature mind. The mature mind knows that the very last thing that will happen is the surprise will be revealed. The mature mind ignores the box. The mature mind explores everything else in the room – and gets much more out of life.

Some people are so obsessed with Death that they idolise him. He hates devotion and believes any deity that needs to be worshipped lacks self-confidence. If a being possesses divine status or power, it knows it is superior to us. He can't comprehend why such an entity would want snivelling, insignificant mortals telling it how wonderful it is all the time. Death compares worship to an amoeba in a fish tank expressing its awe and devotion by swimming towards the light generated by the world's greatest super-computer. He describes praise as a 'one-way shower of emotion directed to those grubby with need'. He is bemused by those of us who throw away our lives on our knees, begging various gods for protection from Death's impending, inescapable grasp. According to him, no god has ever managed, or even attempted to keep a mortal soul from him. He says that only ever happens in storybooks, myths and legends. He despairs of those who waste valuable life-energy pleading into the ether for supernatural assistance. But of course this tale isn't about Death's beliefs, interesting as they are. This tale is about my friend's fling with him.

Although it was my friend's total lack of respect for him that initially caught Death's eye, his attitude changed as soon as they were an item. Once they were courting, he didn't mind her attention. Actually, he liked it. Actually, he loved it. He was quickly enraptured by her being and his desire to be treated with disdain by her evaporated. Conversely, whilst intimately involved, she didn't become obsessed with him. That's not easy to avoid doing; he's a charismatic chap. Where other women would have fallen into the trap of adoration and devotion, she maintained her sense of self. She was never one to be overawed by status, not even that of an immortal entity of immense power. Her ability to remain unchanged while in the closest proximity to his supreme power, enhanced his affection for her.

As well as naturally behaving in an ideal way to keep her partner keen, my friend is incredibly intuitive. She understood what made Death tick; saw the man behind the mask. She saw him as an extraordinary and unique man, rather than a freakish manifestation. And she liked what she saw. She admired, for example, the fact that he worked hard whilst never courting sympathy for the relentless and thankless nature of his job. He didn't live for his work, but never the less, tirelessly got on and did it without complaint. My friend's father had been of the same school of thought. He spent his whole life grafting, never moaning once. She's never been attracted to modern men who bitch and whine. Death was an old-fashioned man's man. Retrosexual, you might say. She did, of course, find his job intriguing. He'd met all the great figures from history after all. But he never once boasted about it. She respected his modesty too. And despite the unpopular nature of his vocation, he was a proud man. Death never appeared ashamed of his role and refused to let the negativity associated with his work affect him. Neither did he ever use his position to threaten or intimidate. He just did the job he had to do. It was his duty, not his obsession. Whilst many saw him as the personification of the act of dying, she saw him for what he was; not what he did — and that's pretty insightful, considering he's spent almost the entirety of eternity shrouded in secrecy.

Mutual admiration and understanding was their bond. Strong glue. Death enjoyed spending time with her, and she with him. And Death truly values time. He knows all too well that good things always come to an end. They revelled. They went out a lot, visited interesting places, went clubbing, and turned up at practically every house party possible. They were very happy together. With regards to their sex life — knowing them both as well as I do — I doubt that was a pedestrian affair. But I'd rather not try picturing what went on under the covers. In summary, they got on like a house on fire, and although he never told me as much, I think he loved her. I don't blame him.

The beginning of the end for their relationship was when my

friend's best friend's son died. He wasn't even two years old. He drowned in the bath. His Mum had dashed downstairs because she remembered she'd left some potatoes boiling on the stove. By the time she got downstairs, the pan had boiled over a bit. She turned the heat down and put the lid on. But starchy potato water was puddled on the hob, so she took a moment to wipe it up. It's always better to wipe up boiled-over starchy potato water before it dries and goes crusty, and sticks to surfaces. For the same reasons, she hastily wiped the outside of the pan too. Then she gave the cloth she'd just used to do the wiping a couple of quick rinses and squeezes under the cold tap. If you don't rinse potato water out of a dishcloth pretty much immediately, it will congeal, turning a once-useful rag into a gooey, unusable clump that you'll never get properly clean again. After doing all that, Mum shot back upstairs to the bathroom. Her baby, who was always so terribly steady in the bath (they had a non-slip bath mat for Christ's sake), was lying face down in four inches of tepid water. He looked like an abandoned girl's doll lying in a wasteland puddle. Mum snatched up her unravelled bundle of joy. He wasn't breathing. She didn't know first aid. Did lots of things wrong. Then called the emergency services. They connected her to a paramedic while an ambulance hurtled towards them. But she kept dropping the phone and was in too much of a panic to clearly follow his instructions. It was probably too late by then anyway. If she had just got one or two things right early on, this would be an entirely different tale. She didn't. It isn't. It's this one.

Death has always said that he's absolutely impartial. He just does his job, no questions asked. He cannot, he claims, make even the tiniest allowance in even the most desperate circumstances. He's seen more pain and anguish than all the warriors of a million-year inter-continental war. He's witnessed, and facilitated, the demise of entire populations and still hasn't let pity divert him from his duty. Death is fundamental to the definition of life and existence. He has to play it by the book. We all understood that. My friend knew it from the start. But sometimes, no matter how much you know something to be true, you hate reality so much that you still fight it. You fight it because particular personal circumstances make a fairness unfair to you. I'm going to divert from the main tale for a moment here and illustrate this point with an example. I need to do this because this very point, defines, and generates the difference between the ideal world and the real world. And this concept is fundamental to appreciating this tale.

Say for example you think it's generally dangerous to drive faster than the speed limit in built-up areas. You feel that people who do this should be punished. But let's say you get caught by a speed-camera that you didn't see because it was deviously obscured from casual view, whilst you were going just a smidgen over a local limit that you weren't even aware of in an area where, on reflection, in your opinion, the set limit is too low. Let's say this happens on a quiet, high-visibility day, at a time at which you have far more important things on your mind than keeping an eye out for randomly selected areas marked out with unnecessarily severe speed limits. Well, if all this did happen to you, you might feel that your fine and the points added to your licence are too much of a punishment; that you've been hard done by. The moment you think that, your life-long belief that it's wrong to drive faster than the speed limit in built-up areas has been shattered. You've been stung by the ideal world/reality schism

– in which the sharp point of reality bursts your bubble of dreamy idealism. That's how my friend felt when her best friend lost her baby. A darling, snugly, giggly little guy was taken away, for ever, from her best friend, by her boyfriend. That's not easy to rationalise. It's even harder to accept.

A deeply empathetic appreciation of her man's career wasn't enough to keep them together. But even faced with the immense challenge of her best friends bereavement, her loyalty may still have held had it not been for one niggling detail. My friend had always suspected that Death had refused to take her at her suicide attempt. She calculated that she should be dead. And she knows what she's talking about when it comes to medical matters. She feels that there were plenty of moments when she should have gone; at the incident site, in the ambulance, in the operating theatre, even in the recovery ward. He's always denied keeping her alive – insisting he maintains absolute integrity at all times. He often explained to sceptical interrogators, that if he started deliberating over marginal cases, for example whether or not to take those who needed just one more second's life to survive something, eventually he'd find it difficult to justify taking those who needed to hang on for two seconds. Rapidly, seconds would become minutes, then minutes would turn into hours. The rule is either stuck to or it isn't. The moment of Death is absolute. He told me he's never saved a life, not since the universe first spawned it. If he did it once, the whole structure of existence as we know it would start disintegrating from that moment. He claimed that if he was ever anything but totally impartial, death would rapidly become impossible to enact. A universe-ending domino effect, with the undermined building blocks of reality collapsing on top of one another in an unstoppable chain reaction, would occur. It is the antithesis of his very essence to save life. He finds the concept abhorrent and asserts that it would be impossible for him to enact.

Now I like the guy, but we have to take his word for it that he never makes exceptions. I mean who's checking up on Death? If I was him; a single guy who could win-over the most wonderful creatures ever created by saving their lives, be their knight in shining armour, I'd twist the rules a little when it suited me. And what greater temptation could there be than a beautiful, charismatic woman like my friend? And what's more, she is bloody clever and if she says she should have died several times, I'm minded to believe her.

The doubts always haunted my once-suicidal friend. Did he refuse to take her? If so, *could* he have held back for just a few moments from taking that toddler? Death is the only one who knows the truth. And, powerful as he is, he can't turn back time. He can't undo his action. He couldn't bring the little boy back to life either. That's outside his remit – someone else's territory.

That infant mortality was the beginning of the end for my friend and Death. The darling couple's relationship was poisoned by the thing that eventually rips all relationships apart – lack of trust. She wanted to believe him, but belief has to be absolute. You can't more or less believe someone. And, as hard as she tried, she couldn't quite believe he hadn't kept her alive whilst emergency medical teams attended to her. And neither was she convinced that he couldn't have spared that little lad. It only took one nail to secure the lid of the coffin she laid their relationship to rest in – a limp eighteen month-old one. A soul searching week or two of after the funeral, my friend did what she felt she had to do. She dumped Death.

People who'd seen them knitted tightly together, but didn't actually know Death that well, thought he might resist her rejection decision and fight for her. He didn't. He took her word as gospel. He accepted it. Once her decree had been announced, he responded with absolute obedience. That's Death all over.

It's been months since they split up, and I haven't been face to face with Death since. I miss him. Love him or hate him – you have to admit his company is pretty stimulating. As for my friend – she hasn't found a new partner. Sometimes I think I should step into the breach and ask her out. Fear of her ex finding out and getting upset isn't putting me off – I know him well enough to know he's not malicious. But the knowledge that he's been with her does disturbs me. I used to marvel at her figure, fantasise about seeing her naked, holding her, having sex with her. But when I think of Death pawing her, touching every square centimetre of her body, contaminating her, I just can't look at her the same way.

THE BEAST OF BEDDGELERT
(PRONOUNCED "BETH-GELUT" –
"GE" AS IN 'GET', "LUT" AS IN 'GLUT')

There's a small town in North Wales, high up amongst the ancient granite mountains of Snowdonia, called Beddgelert. Bedd is the Welsh word for grave – an ominous word that has tainted this isolated settlement for centuries. There was a time when it had a simpler name – plain old Gelert. This tale explains how it earned its alias.

In Gelert there was a fine and noble warrior. Like most of the greatest warriors from history and legend, he was not of noble birth. What he was, was tall, strong, courageous and handsome. His feats impressed men, and his looks impressed women. Applying Post-Modern honesty, his looks also impressed men and his feats also impressed women. But there was more to this hero than beauty and bravery; being raised amongst the hoi polloi gave him a sense of justice often undeveloped among the privileged few he eventually joined. His admirable nature further enhanced his popularity. All classes admire the virtuous.

By the time he was in his late twenties, this impressive character was a noble man with a decent sized estate. He cultivated that land into pastures which yielded bountiful produce. At the centre of his fruitful territory, there was an imposing, well-kept mansion. If you'd seen it, you might have thought it a castle. And yet labouring in the fields of conflict and non-conflict were not this heroic figure's only virtues; he valued and lived for every moment of every day and, in order to maximise on this desire, was incredibly adept at time management. He would spend one third of each year overseeing his productive land – reaping wonderful harvests – and the other two thirds fighting for his King – reaping far more grimly. By the time he'd reached thirty-two, his successes were many. He had turned the tide of many battles, twice saved the life of his monarch, reinvented regional agriculture, improved the situation of the local poor and written celebrated ballads (I forgot to mention he was also an inspirational poet). His deeds did not go unrecognised. At thirty-two, he was made Lord of Gelert. His future seemed rosy.

In nought to thirty-two, he'd gone from nowt to luminary. During those years he'd dedicated himself to worthy causes; his king, his people, learning and literature. He bore a title and the scars of many battles. The one thing he hadn't borne by then, was an heir. For that, he needed a wife. Once he'd set his mind to finding a bride, the Lord of Gelert applied himself to the task with the same dedication he applied to every challenge he'd ever faced. As per usual, he aimed high, setting himself the target of wooing and plucking the fairest flower in the meadow. He found her – a woman whose beauty and bearing blazed like a fiery comet passing in front of a washed-out moon. He captured her heart and she became Lady Gelert. Their love outshone Romeo and Juliet's. Like Orpheus, he would have journeyed to the underworld for her. Like Helen of Troy, twelve-hundred ships weighed low in the water by bronze-armour-wearing and bronze-weapon-bearing troops, could not have compelled her to leave his side.

On the fifth year of their marriage, on the day of his radiant wife's nineteenth birthday, the Lord of Gelert became a father. When he first held his blood-daubed squarbling infant in his scarred and weathered hands, he did something no man, not even his father, could recollect seeing before: he cried. He cried uncontrollably. I'd never dare say it to his face if he were alive, but; he sobbed. In fact, it was worse than that; he blubbed. He blubbed like a three year-old child who's been properly shouted at for the first time in his life. That in itself makes a story, but it's only part of this tale. There's something missing. I've withheld from you a seemingly small detail. Seemingly small, but impactfully seismic. That detail was canine.

As you already know, the Lord of Gelert was a brave, indomitable warrior who no man could match in battle. The only creature to ever equal his courage, was his dog. I say dog, but if you'd seen it, you'd probably think what everyone else thought at the time; that it defied sub-species categorisation being more wolf than any other animal. It was nicknamed 'The Beast'. These well-matched two first met when our human hero, in his mid twenties, had set out to hunt down an infamous wild boar; a vast hog with a ferocious reputation and proven-fatal tusks. It was a monster that bore the scars of many savage battles on its bristly grey hide; like the marks left in drying concrete by a gang of delinquent children armed with pointed sticks. Men and horses had died pursuing this notorious quarry. Slaying it was a challenge the Lord of Gelert could not resist. The fearsome wolf-dog had the same compulsion. No one knows where the hound came from – all we know is that two mighty hunters set out to conquer the terrible boar at the same time – and when our young hero returned from the hunt, emerging from the forest with a bristled bulk of pork

21

slung over his broad shoulders, a like-minded dog, 'The Beast of Gelert', walked to heel beside him.

From that day, up until the point of the Lord's wedding, The Beast never left his master's side. It followed him into battle, ripped limbs off adversaries and sewed fear into the hearts of political opponents. Man and animal were symbiotic. And they were an intimidating pair; both so ominously capable of bloodshed that it was difficult to work out which was most feared − the master or the monster.

Earlier on I implied that nothing ever rippled the waters of Lord and Lady Gelert's mutual devotion. There was one thing: the hound. It didn't like her. It never physically threatened her − The Beast was far too loyal to act in an aggressive way towards his master's wife, but it definitely resented her. On the battlefield or hunt, it took pride of place at his master's side. When they arrived home, it was relegated to second favourite. The Lady of the manor disliked The Beast in equal measure. It frightened her. She could picture it turning on her one day, assaulting her. Whilst she could use her considerable beauty to win over the toughened hearts of her husband's fellow warriors, her celebrated looks meant nothing to The Beast. She imagined she was no more than a piece of meat to it − something to be dismembered and gobbled-down if it was ever given the go-ahead to do so. And she wasn't the only person unsettled by the malignant creature. In fact, the only person who didn't see The Beast as a potential danger, was the Lord of Gelert. After all, it had saved his life several times. It had helped him bring down the most prized quarries and the most ferocious enemies. They were brothers in arms. Before he met his Lady, The Beast was his closest and truest companion. He trusted it absolutely. He knew his wife didn't like his hound – but he put that down to delicate feminine sensibilities.

When the child arrived, things changed again. His one-time best friend was knocked back even further – it now stood third in line for its master's affection. In addition to that injustice, the master started spending more time at home with the family, doing far less of the things they used to enjoy together; namely hunting and fighting. On top of all that, The Beast was growing old. It's hard for a creature that has been defined by its physical prowess to grow older, feebler, more vulnerable. Warmongers like to die in battle; they don't want to carry on to become decrepit and weak and be pushed around by young upstarts. Haunted by it's approaching frailty, the hound developed more attitude than ever. The Lady of Gelert sensed the increasing moodiness of The Beast and it worried her. This ageing four-pawed warrior might turn on her one day, like an elderly cornered rat striking out carefree in the knowledge that the end is fast approaching anyway. She harangued her husband to keep it away from their child. And her husband, loyal firstly to his family, allowed himself to be influenced. Against his heart-felt judgement, he changed the rules. The Beast was not allowed in the same room as the infant. This generally meant that The Beast was ejected from the home altogether. Guiltily, outside, several thick walls from the nearest fire, the Lord of Gelert built his old friend a rude shelter from salvaged materials. It didn't keep out piercing cold winds and it didn't repel driving showers. He had intended to build a magnificent outdoor home; a grand kennel sculpted from fine timber, but his wife's disapproving glares swayed him. The Beast was in the dog house because loyalty to his family had been brought into conflict with loyalty to his canine comrade. This was the first battle our

23

hero didn't know how to win. When the child was eleven months old, the conflict came to a head.

It was the festival of Borain – the patron saint of brotherhood. On this festival it was traditional for a master to in some way trade places with his staff. Because of pride in his lowly heritage and his strong sense of social justice, the Lord of Gelert took this festival to heart. For one night a year, his servants become lords and he became their a servant – he was the original socialist! Every Borain his staff spent the entire afternoon and evening drinking. The lord of the manor was cook and waiter. Chivalry still pervaded though; he wouldn't let his wife roll up her embroidered sleeves, so the Lady of the manor was the glamorous hostess. At around eight on this particular night, dinner was served. Since it was the highlight of the year for the peasant charges, every worker gorged themselves. The centrepiece dish was a whole roasted stag, its huge horns wrapped in silver leaf. Ordinarily, common folk never got to eat venison so they pounced on it like hungry hyenas, devouring as much as they could. Lady Gelert dined with them. Her husband, utterly devoted to the spirit of this festival, refused to consume even a morsel. This decision proved critical. The deer was poisoned. A long-term enemy of the lord of the manor had laced the carcass with poison whilst it hung maturing in the barn. Suddenly everyone started collapsing. Those that had stuffed themselves dropped down dead, others – those who had secured less game meat, began writhing in agony on the floor. The Lord's soul mate, displaying her usual decorum, had swallowed only a small amount of the contaminated flesh – but it was enough to incapacitate her. She displayed similar symptoms to the immobilised mob and as far as the Lord could tell, his true love was about to expire. The worried husband presumed his unpractised culinary skills were to blame for the mass poisoning. Overcome with concern for his wife, he didn't suspect or even consider malicious interference. Honourable men are generally slow to presume deviousness – that is the currency of their corrupt, jealous inferiors. The Lord had only one option to save his wife, he'd have to scoop her up and ride like the wind on his battle charger to the nearest physician. Although he excelled at many things, medicine and antidotes were not amongst them. The only trusted medic lived twenty minutes hard gallop away and he needed to get there rapidly in order to save her. Since he could not travel as quickly carrying both a retching woman and a feeble baby, he decided to leave his son and heir asleep in the castle. Before he did, he rushed outside to fetch his trusty war partner. He hurriedly led it to a room it hadn't entered for nearly a year – the nursery. When they reached that inner sanctum, he dropped to his knees, grabbed two fond fistfuls of wiry fur and flesh, looked into the milky-amber eyes of his ageing thick-coated warrior friend, and said to him; "As you know, that is my boy; my one and only precious child. I will be gone an hour. Protect him, if needs be, with your life." Then, as he exited the room, he stood in the open doorway and added, "I am sorry, great and noble friend, for abandoning you as I have. I will make amends on my return." With this, he turned and left the two together, imagining a new partnership in the making, then hurdled over the dead and dying, and grabbed his wife.

An hour and a half later he returned to the castle. His wife had recovered quickly, having been administered the perfect antidote. They had brought with them the physician and his assistant to save those of the staff who still breathed. Whilst the medicine men set about their business, the Lord and Lady raced to see their beloved child. The child was not there. Neither was The Beast. The cot had been torn apart and the babe's bedclothes were drenched in blood. The large floor-reaching window that looked out onto the lawn had been smashed open. The horrified parents raced out of the newly-made exit and, by the faint light of the moon, saw The Beast. It sat a few strides in front of them proudly licking its bloody chops. Although her husband had the trained reactions of a legendary fighter, the Lord's wife, propelled by ferocious maternal rage, struck first. She launched herself at the smug-looking monster and brought her fist down on its right shoulder blade. Instinctively, as if motivated by some deep-felt pain, it motioned as if to bite the hand that struck it. Before it's jaws had time to clamp together, the Lord was upon it, and his blow was far more damaging than his spouse's. His trusted pet had killed his son and gone for his wife. Anger and mortification drove his powerful left fist down upon the animal's skull like a sledgehammer, knocking the aged monster to the ground. In the same fluid movement, with his right hand the Lord of Gelert drew his dented sword from its scabbard. The dog looked up at him with eyes that said, "Master, I have fought and hunted loyally by your side for over a decade. You have treated me terribly this last year. Do I need to be punished further? I love you Master." The Lord read his old companion's eyes correctly – but ignored them. Fuelled by blinkered wrath, he brought his sword rapidly down. Stricken by loss and mutiny, his blow was far less accurate than usual. It landed off-centre at the upper right side of the hound's forehead, glanced diagonally downwards between its eyes and exited at the left cheek, cutting a clean line across his old friend's snouted face. The mutt's crown was severed like an amateurishly sliced hard-boiled egg, and the askew scalp span off into the night garden like a cheap Frisbee. Silence engulfed the distraught parents. They were alone in the darkness.

Then, in the quiet of the heart-broken night, they heard a sound they immediately recognised. They heard their only child's cry. The cry came from a bush no more than four giant dog-lengths behind where the mutilated hound lay. The Lady of Gelert was so stunned she couldn't move, but the battle-hardened father instantly sprang at the bush. Hidden beneath some hastily assembled branches and leaf matter, camouflaged but not smothered, lay his son. The Lord picked the child up. His blinding rage dissipated. With eyes rapidly adapting to the moonlight, he stood there in his garden, holding his son, taking in more and more of the scene. On the lawn between the bush and the far wall lay two mutilated corpses. He recognised their livery – they wore the distinctive garb of a political opponent.

It became instantly obvious what had happened. This pair, and several others, had been watching the castle to ensure all the occupants died at the feast. When they saw the Lord gallop away, they quickly smashed their way into the castle, straight into the infant's bedroom, charged with infanticide. The moment they entered, the dog was at them before they could swing their swords, biting like a rabid wolf – inflicting savage wounds. The only blow that the slowing Beast received during the first phase of this ambush being a coward's dagger stab to the right shoulder. After this opening melee, the assailants used their overwhelming numbers to charge the cot, but again the creaking monster moved with the speed of a young champion. It leapt in front of them and grabbed the babe by its nightdress, dodging wildly swung blades to carry the tiny child to safety. As the mighty creature evaded the men, one of them, diving towards the cot, could not stop his own momentum and fell upon it, smashing it and coating it with the red juice that ran from a savage bite to his left breast. The dog ran through the open window into the night. By the time the intruders had made it out into the garden and regrouped, the infant was hidden and The Beast was back among them. Without the distraction of protecting a helpless child, it could fight unrestrained. It was in its element. It sprang at the would-be murderers; it tore a hand clean off one; another, it bit the throat out of; and it dug its canines deep into the leg of a further aggressor, splitting a vital artery. It was blood from this wound that The Beast was licking from his lips when his master returned. The brigands were vanquished. Two died on the lawn. Others, some of whom were mortally wounded, fled. The Beast of Gelert would have pursued and killed them all but it thought it more pertinent to guard the child against other potential attackers. For all it knew, that bunch could have been the first of several waves of assailants. So it sat guard. The prudent dog of war had instinctively taken the vulnerable child to where the shadows clouded human eyes. Out there, in the half-dark, with the babe hidden in a bush, it could protect it. It waited its master's return.

There are several old legends that tell the story of how Beddgelert earned its name. They all end somewhere around this point, and they are all wrong. In those versions, the Lord feels awful remorse for his ill-considered act and in response builds a mighty cairn, a distinctive monument to his dog, in order to assuage his guilt. This monument is purported to be the celebrated grave of Gelert, the final resting place of his loyal Beast, and it is claimed the town takes its name from this tomb. But a town never takes its name from a single shrine. Even the great Taj

Mahal fails to dictate the name of the city it is located in. Towns and cities are never named after one mausoleum, no matter how magnificent it is. Human communities are defined by their boundaries, the line at which they are marked out from other places. To properly finish this tale; to undo the Victorian beautification that blanched this and many other meaningful folk tales of their sinister meaning, let me take you back to the moment of stomach-cramping realisation when The Lord of Gelert grasped the terrible nature of his error.

The careless master stood in his dark garden, holding his rescued fledgling, whilst he pieced together the likely events of the battle that had taken place while he was away. He pictured his dog savaging the assassins. He smiled. It reminded him of all the glorious hunts and wars they'd survived together before the helpless child had arrived. Then he looked at the infant's eyes. They had the crystalline sparkle of his mother's. He knew that every time he looked at those eyes he'd be reminded of the boy's mother. And he knew that every time he pictured his wife, his thoughts would dwell on the way he'd allowed her to convince him to abandon his trusty canine companion. Without a word he handed the baby to his mother. Then he walked over to where his shaggy friend's body lay, picked it up, and slung it over his left shoulder. He strode a few paces away from the castle, stopped, and turned back. His wife thought that, after momentarily thinking of leaving his family, he was coming back to her. He wasn't. He walked back to where the lopped-off section of his hound's skull had landed, picked it up, then turned and walked off into the night forest, tightly gripping the chunk of roughly-hewn flesh and bone in his bloodied fist, like a Templar Knight clasping the Holy Grail. He didn't once look back to his home, to his wife, to his only child.

The Lord of Beddgelert was never seen again. The man who sponsored the murderous plot against his family went missing within a few weeks. As did his wife. And his three sons. And his five healthy grandchildren. In the months that followed, the two brothers of the plotter, and his two sisters, several nephews and nieces, and his favourite horse, disappeared too. Whilst complete corpses were never found, they found bits of bones together with various scraps of clothing and jewellery that indicated who the deceased owners were.

The various bits and pieces of bodily remains didn't prove a hazard to health. There was no flesh on them to putrefy and stink, and spread disease – just dry, white bones stripped clean of flesh. With human tooth marks gouged into them. And no evidence of cooking. No one had the courage, or the foolhardiness, to afford the pitiful remaining scraps a decent burial. All the townsfolk dared do was drop a chunk of rough granite to indicate each final resting place – an unmarked tombstone that couldn't be traced to its sculptor. Before the disappearances ceased, some thirty odd man-placed stones appeared in the countryside surrounding Gelert. Join together those nervously offloaded boulders on a map, and you'll draw the parish boundary of Beddgelert. So although 'Bedd' does mean grave, it refers not to the grave of one celebrated hero, but to the many graves of many tragic victims. This is the true story of how Beddgelert earned its name.

FEELING MYSELF
PART I

My journey towards self-discovery began when I finished with Melanie after swallowing the last mouthful of the dinner she'd cooked me for my fortieth birthday. The meal had been fine, and had been accompanied by a decent claret, but I felt ready for a change of personal circumstances. In response she stood up, grabbed the wine bottle by the neck, smashed its end off against the edge of the table, and thrust it into my face. As it struck, she twisted it anti-clockwise, the razor-sharp jagged edges turning like a savage kaleidoscope. If you'd peered down the neck of that bottle as she ground it into me, you would have expected to see wild patterns form in fresh blood and shredded flesh. My blood. My flesh. There weren't any patterns. There wasn't any blood. I did feel an irritating circular scratching sensation, but my skin wasn't broken. I was annoyed by her attack though. Burgundy coloured wine had splattered everywhere, and ugly misshapen shards of green glass littered the shiny white-tiled floor. Mess upset me. It always had. Melanie knew that and had even accused me several times of suffering from neatness OCD. I asked her to leave.

As soon as she'd gone, I tidied up the broken glass and mopped up the spilt wine. When that crime scene had been scrubbed clean, I tackled another – the kitchen. As usual, pots, pans, crockery and cutlery littered every surface. Her housekeeping skills were as refined as those of a bunch of children playing mummies and daddies. Once again she'd left a couple of near-empty pans on the ceramic hob as it cooled down. The food left in them had dried hard and stuck like roadpaint while we tucked into our meal. How she never worked out the implications of leaving pans like that, I'll never know. Scraping hard-set former foodstuff from the bottom of the soiled pans assured me I'd made the right decision to send her packing. She hadn't actually packed. Her dirty underwear still resided in my linen basket, her toothbrush still stood to attention next to mine in the wall-mounted jar in the bathroom, and her trusty jar of jerk seasoning still looked out of place among the uniform bottles in my spice rack. Those things were easily dealt with. After washing-up, I boxed up all her possessions, purged my home of evidence of her ever being there, removed her from my past. The one trace of her I didn't remove was the sheet on my bed, which still bore physical and olfactory evidence of her presence. Since her crazed behaviour had denied me penetrative pleasure that night, I'd have to resort to masturbatory gratification. Those reminders of our lust would help that activity feel less solitary.

The following morning I went to Le Boulangerie and collected a baguette for breakfast. For the record, my local bread shop was not a boulangerie, you find them in France. But the owner; an American who, in a French accent, constantly espoused the superiority of Gallic baking – did produce exemplary breads and pastries. The delightful freshness of his wares just outweighed the tedious experience of being exposed to his transparent affectations. That morning my mood must have been a little heavy because he allowed me to escape relatively quickly, untraumatised by his effusive Franglais. I emerged from his shop, French stick under my arm, a bachelor marching to my own tune again, and strode on to the Italian deli where I picked up a jar of seedless raspberry jam. Melanie had used the last spoonfuls of my previous jar in the sponge-sandwich birthday cake she'd made me. By the time I was busy birthday-gift raping myself on my cum-stained purple bed sheet, that cake was already being broken down by the stomach acids of the latchkey dogs that hung out in my backyard. I'd never been big on birthday cakes, or, for that matter, birthdays. Their approach always filled me with apprehension – a sense that another soon-to-be-lost year was reaching a cataclysmic end. I'd always felt that the passing of a year of life should be mourned, not celebrated. I tried to remember a birthday that I'd actually enjoyed, and not one came to mind. Being stabbed in the face by a woman I was hoping to have break-up sex with, however, was a first. And I couldn't let it go. My ability to concentrate on day-to-day life was affected.

Back at my pad, as I carved thick slices of crusty bread in my re-sanitised kitchen, my attention kept being drawn to my left forearm. In some ways it was like a baguette; light brown, hard, ovoid in cross-section. I imagined how different it must appear on the inside – red, fibrous, muscular tissue rather than the white, soft, spongy, elastic crumb produced by the tiresome Francophile. My curiosity transformed into investigative action before I'd cut enough slices of bread for my breakfast. I pressed the near-end of the breadknife's serrated blade against the upper side of my forearm halfway between wrist and inner elbow, and dragged the sharp even-toothed edge with force and purpose along my submissive limb. I wanted to see the bloody tissue that Melanie's

33

attack had failed to reveal. But my curiosity was not sated. Once again, my flesh refused to tear. I knew that wasn't normal. I shuffled bemused to my breakfast bar, and sat for a while switching the focus of my vision between five centimetre slices of French-style loaf, and my unmarked arm. I tried to remember the last time I had torn my flesh and seen inside myself.

My earliest clear memory of bleeding profusely was when I'd tripped as a ten year old, running with a bamboo cane in my mouth. I'd been pretending I was an Amazonian hunter with a blow pipe. Blood gushed from my throat that day. I thought I was going to die and was convinced Dad should have phoned for an ambulance. But he calmly sat me on the draining board, seemingly unconcerned by the possibility of me dying, and told me to lean over the sink; grumbling that my blood had ruined the carpet. A very expensive carpet, he hastened to add – as if the carpet was more precious than his only son. However unsettling that childhood memory was, it was of no use in helping understand the inner me. I needed to investigate lasting evidence of previous breaks in my skin; scars. So, as its impossible to stare clearly down the back of one's own throat, I tried to recollect other major cuts that would have left lasting observable scars. I remembered one I'd received in the Alps during my early twenties. I'd gone to spend the summer with a friend who worked all year round at a ski resort. During the summer months, the hotels of the resort were filled with those interested in snowless mountain activities. My friend was working in the largest hotel in the resort – a concrete monolithic blight on the picturesque surroundings. His job was to empty the rubbish bins. One particularly busy day, there was a changeover of guests and he had lots of work to do. He wasn't going to be free until the evening, and

I've always hated wasting a day, so I decided to set out on a hike alone. I needed to shake off a few cobwebs so planned a decent trek, an eight-hour circular route linking together a few peaks in the vicinity. My friend had no maps, but insisted the route was established and easy to follow. Largely speaking he was right and I enjoyed several hours of easy-to-navigate dramatic scenery and mountain air. The fun stopped when I got lost descending from the final, and highest, peak. After that zenith, all that was left was a long descent to the resort. I became blasé after reaching it and, keen to join my mate for a well deserved beer, began heading drinkwards in a reckless manner. Youthful arrogance convinced me there would be countless paths joining this imposing landmark and the thriving community below. That, I realised to my peril, was foolhardy naivety. I think I lost the path pretty much the moment I set off from the peak. From then on, using left-on lights in hotel rooms as my lodestars, I found myself heading further and further off-piste. They were cruel beacons, acting like the glowing lures of an angler fish. The closer I got to them, the more imperilled my journey became, as my descent grew ever steeper. From about halfway between summit and sustenance, the rough grasses and ankle-high scrub of the relatively uniform higher slopes turned to thigh-high foliage draped over sudden drops of ten feet or more. As I made my way along this rough terrain, night was threatening to descend more quickly than me. The threat of impending unavigable blackness made turning around and heading back up the steep mountainside in the hope of finding the main path, a less favourable option than pressing on. So I struggled forwards and downwards, gripping clumps of foliage as organic handrails to steady myself as I navigated giant's steps and loose-boulder mantraps. As I was doing

35

so, I convinced myself that those dangerous conditions were as bad as it was going to get. Then, when I seemed to be no more than half a mile from the resort – almost close enough to smell the yeasty European lager – my journey was abruptly halted. I had come to the top of an expansive cliff face. I looked over the edge; there was a two hundred metre drop. Climbing down at the point I had met it would have been way too dangerous. I looked to the left for a break in its severity, and it continued as far as I could see. A long, cruel, imposing vertical face stretched away into the distance. The same view was repeated to my right. I froze for a few precious minutes of daylight to calculate the wisest course of action; and became a stone statue atop a mighty castle's battlements.

The necessity for action reanimated me. The best thing to do was to find somewhere to climb down the face. I had done a little climbing, so knew techniques that would help. Admittedly, all my climbing up until then had involved a climbing partner, ropes, harnesses, helmets and sticky boots. On that occasion I found myself equipped with much less specialised equipment: a pair of tennis shoes, jeans, a light-grey lightweight Adidas waterproof jacket and a daysack stuffed full of useless bits and pieces. Nevertheless, down-climbing still felt like the best choice – as long as I could find a safe enough route. I headed left along the cliff top, the direction that seemed to offer more opportunities for a scree slope or vegetated ravine. But after fifty metres of struggling along overgrown, jagged, uneven cliff top, I had second thoughts, and retraced my route. I anxiously passed the point at which I'd come to the cliff, and continued past it. A hundred metres of even harder going told me two things: I was starting to panic and make rash decisions, and I should have trusted my initial instinct. So, telling myself out loud that I was gaining control of the situation, I once again retraced my steps, orally committing myself to head purposefully in the original direction until a reasonable opportunity to descend the cliff face presented itself. With changing birdsong heralding the fast-approaching night, I knew I wasn't as in control as I was trying to convince myself I was, and that I'd likely throw myself at the first half-decent chance to get off that mountain. That chance was a corner formed where two sections of the cliff face met at an angle of around one hundred and twenty degrees. Although two sprawling cliff faces meeting at such a wide angle might not seem to offer much hope of a descent, gentle macro-geological features often create much more extreme effects up close. In this case, a crack had formed at the convergence. It averaged around a metre wide, cut three metres into the rock face, and appeared to run all the way to ground level. I decided that the fissure would be my fire escape, my opportunity for a rapid descent.

Halfway down the two-hundred metre crack, I realised that from the moment I'd left the peak of the mountain, I'd been spiralling in ever diminishing circles towards my own destruction. One hundred metres above the ground, the crack narrowed abruptly. It shrank from being wide enough to wriggle my body down to the width of my fist. The narrowing didn't go on for too long; five metres or so – but for that distance, I would have to emerge from the relative safety of the crack and climb down the cliff face; tired, fragile, petrified, alone. I had no choice. Retracing footsteps was no longer an option. At that point, I was still wearing the small rucksack containing useless accessories; a bottle of water, some chocolate bars, a spare jumper, a flask of tea, sunglasses, a book of short stories and my camera. Although it didn't weigh that much, I didn't want the extra burden of a bag dragging me backwards as I edged out onto the face. So I threw it below, down to the grey scree which, from that height, looked like the track ballast of a toy railway. As my rucksack plummeted downwards, swerving a little in the wind, I noticed how silent the mountain was. Enveloped in its granite folds, I was shielded from the evening birdsong (which at the time I imagined had ceased in reverence to my plight), and all I could hear was a light gambolling of the wind. The instant the bag hit the rugged ground, the air inside it was puffed out – as my lungs would have been if I'd followed its path. The sudden constriction caused it to explode silently open and spew its miserable contents in all directions. Bagless and helpless, I edged backwards out of the crack, and began to climb down the narrow fault line by sticking my feet in it and reaching deep into it with my arms. I used that grubby crack like an awkward, rungless, rope ladder. As I neared the bottom of the thin section, it widened again beneath me - a marvellous sight. I could see that it stayed wide enough, all the way to my rucksack's ground zero, to enable me to tuck back inside and descend far less perilously. But, as I tried to edge my lower body into the wider fissure, hands clasped around two rock-dust coated nodules in the narrow crack above, the unsuited-to-extreme-climbing plastic soles of my tennis shoes failed me. Both feet slipped, and my legs swung out. I was an unseated knight's squire, lacking the protective armour of his master. I felt myself momentarily hovering, treading-air at the top of the fall that would certainly kill me. Then I began falling earthwards.

My swollen-through-fatigue-and-fear left forearm saved me. Half a metre into my death plunge, arms rattling down the crack like potatoes dropped down a drainpipe, hands rendered useless by the speed of descent, my forearm slid into a final further constriction of the crack. It became wedged like a cork in a wine bottle, providing me with an instant anchor. My fall was abruptly halted as I slammed into the vertical rock. It was excruciatingly painful, but I didn't care. I regained my footing and, with great difficulty, managed to prize the stuck arm free before shakily resuming a more controlled descent. The wedging and the prizing had gouged a ten centimetre long, one centimetre deep tear in my forearm. As I descended the last ninety-five metres of cliff, snuggled inside the crack like a petrified rat, that cut rained blood all over me like a watering can fitted with a rose spout. And, as is always the way with wounds sustained during inescapable strenuous activity, it hoovered-up grit and grime at the same time. When I reached the bottom, my contaminated wound still oozing claret, I jogged to my exploded rucksack's contents. To settle my nerves I took the lid off my ejected flask and poured myself a calming cup of tea. The tea and glass cocktail that slopped out into the plastic screw-on cup reminded me that I was not thinking straight. My thoughts switched to my medical needs and I turned to my water bottle to wash the filth out of my cut. But that bottle was glass too, and had suffered the same fate as the flask. Unrefreshed and uncleansed, shaking with fear and pain, I gathered-up my remaining scattered possessions and charged onwards to the nearest stream to clean the wound. Desperate to feel less isolated and vulnerable, I filled the void of by-then sleeping birds by screaming out loud that I'd never go near a cliff again.

By the time I got the resort it was dark. It had seemed much closer from the top of the cliff than it actually was. The only doctor in residence had taken the night off and the single remaining trained medical person was my mate's snowboarding buddy – an ex auxiliary nurse who'd abandoned low-level medicine five years earlier to live in the mountains. His new occupation was serving drinks in the resort's wildest bar. He offered to stitch the wound for me; so my mate and I drank ourselves stupid – me out of necessity, and him out of solidarity. The ex-nurse did a good job, using the bar owners' sewing kit. She was a needlework hobbyist so had plenty of good quality thread to hand. I'd bled plenty that day, then had to pull the wound open to rinse out ingrained filth, and then wait two hours after arriving at the resort before I'd necked enough Sambucas to endure the pain of minor surgery. That day was unforgettable and I had the scar to prove it.

Trouble is, I didn't. Though I could clearly remember strumming that scar like a banjo string as I headed home on the train at the end of that summer, not a trace of the injury remained. That's not how scars are meant to work. They should be permanent reminders of wounds. I tried to remember when I'd last seen the scar, but realised I couldn't. I'd always sensed my memories were somehow a bit peculiar. In them, I rarely seemed to be entirely me. In fact, they seemed to feature a variety of different mes. I'd previously rationalised this, thinking everyone probably feels that way. But, post bottle-smash-morning, a day over forty and covered in skin tougher than a shark's, I finally accepted that there was something particularly odd about me. I needed definitive evidence, so grabbed a nail gun from my tool cupboard, placed my hand on the wooden cutting board I'd just sliced my French stick on, and fired a nail into the back of my hand. It stung a little, made a pointed dent in my flesh, but didn't penetrate. That result proved it beyond any possible doubt. My skin's virtual impenetrability was in an altogether higher order of oddness than my memories seeming a bit funny. I knew for certain that I was *very* different to everyone else; and I determined to find out why.

HUMAN ABATTOIR REPORT

They've made numerous improvements at the abattoir since my last inspection. Many of the improvements have been technological. Those alone are admirable displays of invention and industriousness worthy of note. But I am even more impressed by the considerable efforts put into raising the living standards of those awaiting slaughter. Starting, though, with scientifically quantifiable considerations, the biggest technological achievement is the new tasteless anaesthetic. Gourmet chefs and gastronomes around the world have made taste comparisons between produce from anaesthetised and non-anaesthetised culls. I'm delighted to report that not one single judge has discerned a noticeable difference in taste. There is, however, a drawback with the technique required to administer the new drug. At present, this tasteless medicine is much more easily absorbed into cellular material than the detectable alternatives. As a consequence, the anaesthetic has to be delivered gradually, but directly into the largest available volume of moving blood. No artery presents the required conditions since injecting it intravenously causes local anaesthesia, without the desired subsequent general anaesthesia. This problem is resolved by drip feeding this advanced chemical directly into the right ventricle of the heart. Since the entire blood volume needs to be slowly infused, it takes around eighty minutes to produce fully incapacitating anaesthesia via this method. This is roughly twenty times longer than required for effective delivery of the most widely available low-taste option via intravenous delivery. The most obvious practical downsides of this new method, are the mildly traumatic act of inserting the needle into the heart of the donor and the need for passive cooperation whilst the anaesthetic takes full effect. Being an invasive procedure, the insertion does cause some discomfort. This cannot realistically be avoided so the recipient requires a coaching programme prior to the procedure. Additionally, during the time that the process is underway, there is a risk that a previously compliant individual will 'freak out' which can result in damage to equipment and even halt the procedure. The greatest challenge, however, is not technical; it is obtaining cooperation from the donor in the first instance. And although this does require highly-trained employees to exact, from my seasoned perspective, this humane method of tasteless neutralisation requires little more collaboration from the slaughtee than many of the more established methods of extinguishment.

There are of course critics of the need for this new method. In my opinion, these represent the 'if it ain't broke don't fix it' lobby. Such people always resist the new. Their conjecture is, if you are going to go to the trouble of spending expensive man-hours grooming willing participants to cooperate, you'd be better off devoting that same expense and energy convincing them to agree to being extinguished by tried and tasted anaesthetic-free mechanical methods. This group of detractors is also vocally suspicious of exactly how willing participants in this technique are. There is some justification to this argument. Although the public can see that this new anaesthetic results in participants arriving at the ceasing centre completely incapacitated; they don't know what prior trauma has taken place in the prepping rooms away from public scrutiny. I predict these Luddites will shrink in number as the method becomes more widely used in the sector, and the supply of affordable pure-tasting meat product increases.

The main fiscal problem I see with this method, is the degree of expertise required to administer it. Very detailed heart rate and blood pressure readings must be taken to make sure that the subject is anaesthetised correctly. Releasing the anaesthetic too slowly can cause the subject to experience complete motor-paralysis without brain-function anaesthesia. If this occurs, the slaughtee will experience their own butchering without the ability to express any distress – detail of which, should it leak out, would be manna from heaven to the critics. On the other hand, if the anaesthetic is administered too quickly, this potent chemical stops the heart; leaving abattoir workers with a lifeless corpse of zero value. Should this occur, standby ECG teams are on hand to offer life support for long enough to get the patient to the ceasing rooms. But this is expensive. And the idea of reviving a carcass only to neutralise it again, confuses the consuming public.

On the positive side, considerable numbers of slaughtees have elected to join this programme. Whilst these figures are undoubtedly influenced by hugely generous incentives made available to dependants, I am concerned that the considerable level of investment necessary to achieve this upturn is not sustainable in the long term. However, I am confident that, with the right support and as, inevitably, the cost per head comes down, tasteless anaesthesia has a strong, secure future. Concluding on the subject, I would say that further development is needed. The concept of tasteless general anaesthesia is a noble and potentially paradigm-shifting one. However, this is still a procedure in its infancy.

There are other new technological advances that have been introduced since my last inspection. These include the ingenious use of strobing lights and moving surfaces to disorientate aggressive resisters. Here, subjects are directed into padded rooms that have a hydraulically-operated floor, ceiling and walls. The walls are laced with bright computer-controlled halogen spotlights. Shifting the surfaces, whilst flashing the lights in programmed sequences, has proven effective in temporarily pacifying seventy percent of hostiles of all grades. The level of disorientation and debilitation can turn a violent non-compliant into a B-One-Plus acceptor. Other notable advances are in the area of annulment. When I started inspecting abattoirs twenty-plus years ago, some of the methods of extinguishment were, with the benefit of hindsight, a little clumsy. At the time, we all acknowledged that staff were going to great pains to make the final act as serene as possible. Compared to where we now are, I am compelled to say that some of the early approaches were bordering on the brutal. It is worth acknowledging that this is an emotive business. Ending the life of another human is always going to be polemical. What we therefore have to ensure is that witnesses in the galleries are exposed to as little detectable distress as possible. The best way to make ceasing palatable to the amateur spectator is to make the act of termination as serene as possible. My favourite new method of cessation involves firing a flat-headed barbed dart into the spinal column of the slaughtee at the back of the neck. This is administered from behind from an ingeniously designed neck brace. The brace is fitted in a specialist prep room equipped with the fitting machinery and ancillaries. In this room, MRI technology is employed to ensure that the dart release point is precisely positioned between two vertebrae. The brace (or 'necklace', as abattoir workers prefer to describe it) can still be used when slaughtees make moderate efforts to resist. This is because the collar (as I prefer to describe it) is fitted tightly in order to keep the dart accurately aligned. The tightness around the neck has the useful side effect of pacifying the wearer by restricting the flow of oxygen to the brain. Still, even this collar cannot be used on subjects rated as highly agitated, exceptionally strong or aggressively resistant, as they are likely to sufficiently dislodge the clinical fitting in order to render it useless. Other new techniques of neutralisation include: methods of reverse defribulation that cause less muscle spasms and so avoid the associated flesh-toughness of previous approaches; and addictive accumulative poisons that dissipate from the product within a few days of slaughter.

Whilst all these advances are to be celebrated, it saddens me that so much of our focus is always drawn to the act itself. It makes me think of first-time mothers who worry more about the birth of the child they are carrying, than how they intend to raise it over the following eighteen years. Whilst annulment has always attracted huge levels of interest, invention and investment, it is the opinion of this Chief Senior Inspector that this skewed focus is the result of people thinking with their hearts rather than their heads. Allowing this to happen causes social and scientific energy to be invested to a degree considerably out of proportion with what informed interest in the general needs of the slaughtees would effect. These hapless individuals are generally far more concerned with the conditions of their stay at a facility *prior* to the moment of their cessation than they are about the nature of the final act. The governor at Walthamstow is of the same mind.

I am therefore proud to report that considerable and noticeable advancement has occurred in the field of slaughtee care over the last twenty-four months in particular. This is the period over which the new holding wing has been in operation. When I first entered the new wing, I could have been forgiven for imagining I had entered a holiday resort! Slaughtees therein live out their last months in considerable comfort. The standard and variety of food on offer has dramatically improved. They are provided with mod cons such as computer gaming, intranet data access, luxurious fixtures and fittings, on demand music (from a carefully chosen selection) and a private en suite toilet. And that's just the basic package. Day to day life is further improved for compliant slaughtees. Well-behaved inmates are allowed to exercise for up to two hours a day. Most of them take up this opportunity. Up until the final detox fortnight, residents are even allowed a modest ration of alcoholic beverages.

Among all this new thinking, the innovation that has truly impressed me, is an allowance for a limited number of visitors. This one change is almost solely responsible for a revolutionary increase in slaughtee cooperation. As you know, I have campaigned for a long time for the better treatment of slaughtees, maintaining that doing so is our best weapon against those trying to undermine state-endorsed cannibalism. Whilst the purpose of this report is not to regurgitate the legal righteousness of the consumption of these individuals, when it comes to the benefits of high standards of care, the proof of the pudding is most definitely in the eating. The Walthamstow Abattoir is undeniably proving that treating slaughtees as people reaps considerable, detectable, quantifiable benefits. In just two years, compliance rates in this modern centre have risen by twenty-seven percent across the board. Reported violent resistance is down nineteen percent. Electively subjugated cessation has risen by a remarkable forty percent.

Without intending any disrespect to previous governors (who have perhaps operated during more challenging times), the present governor is a visionary; an admirable leader and a dedicated humanitarian. In the last two years, under his direction, client care standards have improved more than in any previous two – or, dare I say it; five-year period! His words and actions demonstrate his absolute commitment to the guardianship and welfare of those in his care. The residents of the Abattoir have even given him a nickname – The Shepherd. He looks after his flock. The successes of the new wing have even spilled over into the surrounding ones, with performance yardsticks rising throughout the complex. Even the mentors are happier, knowing that their clients are getting a richer experience.

I also believe that operating an intern-focused centre such as the new wing, producing quality uninterfered-with natural product, undermines the growing passion for wild meat. The benefits of this new establishment nullify many of the claimed justifications of those extolling the benefits of wild meat. The new wing offers a pleasant existence right up to the point of cessation. Attendees are taking exercise, keeping their flesh in good condition. Some are even attending the spa where treatments are specifically designed to improve the quality of the end product. Perhaps the most resounding illustration of the success of the present governor's methods is the fact that friends and relatives visiting during the final months are pre-ordering product derived from their own loved ones. I have met several (and heard of many more) family members and close companions who have ordered prime organic product from their interned associate prior to his or her cessation. And if that doesn't say everything about a rise in standards of the conditions of the slaughtees and the corresponding improvements in the quality and flavour of the product, I don't know what does! In fact, for dinner tonight, I am eating rump-steak from a particularly attractive female in her early-thirties with whom I carried out several private interviews over my monitoring period. Not only did she encourage me to consume some of herself once butchered, but she also carried out a tailored exercise regime to ensure that her arse was of the highest possible culinary standard. The quality of her living conditions had made her feel empowered enough to study human gastronomy and oenology during the wait for her number to come up. As a tribute to her; the regime she has blossomed in; and her inspirational governor, I will shortly stop typing and raise my glass to her arse. On her express advice, I will be drinking a very expensive Pouilly-Fumé to accompany a fricasseed chunk of her rear, served over wild rice, with sautéed celeriac and steamed mange tout. Honourable colleagues; dinner has now arrived. I hereby conclude my report.

Buon appetito!

UBP©

Five years ago, they started selling Utter Beauty Paint – or UBP©. It's by far the most expensive thing per unit weight you can buy. We all knew it was on its way. They'd been talking it up for years. The first thing we heard was reports of the concept. Then came news of the existence of an early prototype formula. Next we were told they'd perfected it, but it would never be affordable. Finally, press leaks said it would be affordable – but only to the very rich. It was the most eagerly anticipated development since lost limb regeneration was cracked twenty-eight years ago.

The minute I heard it would eventually go on general sale, I began saving for some UBP©. Every month I put twenty percent of my monthly wages into shares of Aphrodite (the company that owns the patent), presuming my desire for their product would be universal. My faith in it, and the impregnability of the patents, was rewarded. UBP© did everything it promised to and the shares rocketed. Six months ago, more thanks to the immense growth of the company's value than to my modest investment, I cashed in my shares and bought five millilitres of UBP©. That snivelling amount was enough to coat, with a thin veneer, a small wooden flower I'd bought for the purpose. The following morning, a Saturday, I gave my girlfriend that painted flower in her kitchen, whilst her parents took breakfast in the next room. She was overawed by its beauty. Although she'd seen the odd example of absolute beauty in shops and galleries, she never thought she'd actually *possess* something of unquestionable beauty herself. I don't know what she was most impressed by; the flower, or my ability to provide her with something so breathtakingly beautiful. Whatever the overriding impulse, her response was to suck my cock there and then – her head moving rapidly back and forth like a metronome set to 'vivacissimo'. After she'd gulped back the last dollop of my love-cream, she asked me to marry her. I accepted. I hope you'll agree that I displayed admirable forethought in both the way I appropriated and utilised my miniscule quantity of UBP©.

Amongst the lower social codes, it's not necessarily the amount of UBP© we appropriate that marks us out from the crowd; it's as much how we use it that counts. The super-rich buy it in volume – they paint themselves. In their wealthy households, in mirrors and marital beds, they are constantly bombarded with sublime examples of human beauty. They live constantly surrounded by magnificent forms – like the offspring of Zeus in Olympus. I'd find that level of exposure distracting to the extent that it would consume me; render me useless. If my girlfriend was the most beautiful creature imaginable, I'd never leave her side. I'd want to be absorbed in her every moment; watch every conceivable play of light on her as she moved through each day. I'd want to watch her as she rose in the morning, yawned her way through breakfast, worked, scratched her arse, bathed, dined, drank, urinated, puked. Compelled by the desire to continually revel in her glory, I'd limpet myself to her. And this desire for attachment would be compounded by the fact that I wouldn't trust anyone else with her. I'd be convinced that if I left her alone for a few minutes, some scoundrel would be trying to get a piece of her. My girlfriend is pretty, don't get me wrong. But pretty is to absolute beauty, like a mewling new-born Persian kitten is to the roaring leader of the fiercest pride of lions in Africa. They might both be felines, but in every other sense they couldn't be more different. I've heard tales of select parties in the most privileged sectors at which all the guests are divinely beautiful. That must be an incredible sight to witness. I often wonder how their servants deal with exposure to such omnipresent dazzling beauty. Perhaps they only manage to do so by constantly reminding themselves that their time amongst the demigods is like a waking dream; that they will be returning to ugly, everyday reality as soon as their shift finishes. The same is not true for the gilded ones. They are permanently confronted by perfect human forms. Surrounded by limitless beauty, and with incredible wealth taken for granted, the supremely wealthy must be the only people on this planet who don't fall for good looks. With immaculate appearance guaranteed by UBP©, and affluence taken for granted, they must fall in love with people for who they actually are, not what they look like. That tickles me. The über-rich, who have traditionally been empowered to be the most fussy about the appearance of their amours, are suddenly the only class to be free of this concern. I'd love to be in their situation; not super rich and constantly surrounded by completely beautiful human specimens – that would be tiresome – but wholly focused on what someone is like on the inside. That has to be the ideal goal when choosing a partner. When I was in my late teens, I had a female friend who was great company. We used to hang out together all the time. She was funny, interesting, kind and loving. But my goodness she was ugly. And I don't mean minor-league ugly – she was a mampee. She had a face like a loose-jowled, grumpy warthog with bad skin chewing on a mouthful of angry wasps mixed with cat shit. We got on so well that if she'd been even half decent looking I'd have married her. She wasn't. I didn't. Although I believe in the ideal of falling for someone's personality, is does not make me wish I had inordinate wealth, because strangely, UBP© hasn't brought the super rich happiness. They are as miserable as the rest of us. Whilst we rack our brains for ways of obtaining as much UBP© as we can get our hands on, they are haunted by the constant fear of one day being unable to continue to afford it in volume. If that happened, their lives would rapidly turn very ugly. They'd plummet from the dizzy heights of aesthetic and financial fulfilment to find their feet on plain old common ground. Their anxiety might be different – but it's anxiety nonetheless.

When UBP© was launched, they marketed it as 'Optical Ambrosia'. They promised it had the potential to make us all happier by offering mortals an opportunity to glimpse Heaven. But all 'miracle' inventions have their side effects. And the rule of thumb with life-changing technologies is the more we submit ourselves to their absolute necessity, the more freedom we sacrifice. Rather than enhancing our lives, UBP© has enslaved us. It has become the focus of all our lives, no matter what strata of society we belong to. It is our obsession. What promised to delight us, now defines us. The only way to be truly happy since the launch of UBP©, is to be immune to it. If you could be inoculated against its effects, or wear glasses that enabled you to see straight through it, you'd once again see the world as it really is. You'd no longer be sucked into UBP©'s overpowering socio-commercial dominance. You wouldn't behave abnormally when confronted with it. You wouldn't yearn for as much exposure to it as you could possibly get. You wouldn't make extreme sacrifices just to get a few drops of it. You wouldn't spend half your life preoccupied by it, craving it, marvelling at its power. I long for the day someone develops an antidote which frees us from our grotesque addiction. If that ever happens, I hope it'll be distributed to everyone, regardless of wealth. Everyone except my wife, that is. She loves that little wooden flower.

GENGHIS BROWN

I'm a rat. A Common Rat. A Brown Rat. Rattus norvegicus. My species' lot is pretty shitty at the moment. So I've been thinking hard about developing an evolution solution. You probably perceive evolution as a gradual process – backed-up by pictures of monkeys on the way to being men; fish growing limbs and dinosaurs getting nastier. Evolution isn't a gradual process. That's why they never find missing links. Evolution occurs in jumps. Here's an example. Some antelope-type-creature is born with freakishly long horns. These horns offer no great assistance to survival and actually weigh the creature down as it tries to escape a lion. The long-horn gene isn't passed on. Some antelope-type-creature is born with a freakishly long neck which enables it to reach nutritious leaves that all the others can't. This extended vertebral section doesn't present any extra vulnerability. Hey presto, you're catapulted in giraffe territory. Study the subject more deeply and you'll discover there's more to it than that. Rather than wait for freak mutation to deal you a lucky hand, you can proactively encourage and shape your own evolutionary development. All it takes is a bit of insight and then careful management. In layman's terms, evolution is a bit like establishing a relationship – someone's got to make the first move – someone has to grasp the nettle. If you fancy someone – ask them out on a date. If you fancy evolving, you need to engineer a way to purposefully nudge evolutionary forces in the right direction. And there's no area of evolution where benefits are more quickly reaped than symbiosis. And the most successful area of all the examples of symbiotic evolution in the history of life on earth is domestication. Take dogs. They came from wolves. And look at them now; distributed all over the globe in all sorts of shapes and sizes. They strut round like they're the most savvy animals ever – 'Check out me. I'm a dog. I hang out with humans. We got together way back when they were still slumming it in caves. Aren't we the cleverest.' Canine pampering is a multi-billion dollar industry. They've even got film stars. Man's best friend. Well in my book, the clever ones aren't the dogs of today who walk to heel and obey silent whistles. It's the wolves that first chose to ally themselves with human hunters that I *really* admire. It must have taken exceptional intelligence to forge that early relationship. Back then, men would have hunted or hidden from wolves. Yet those lupines calculated that there were advantages to being near men. This was an insight they could, and did, pass on to their pampered descendants.

Whilst dogs have a pack of pioneering wolves to whom they should feel eternally grateful, they aren't the only beneficiaries of domestication. Plenty of other animals have done well out of mixing with humans. Cats are the other obvious contenders. For personal reasons, I find it hard to sing the praises of their early ancestors but, objectively, I have to say early wild felines played an even better hand than the wolves. Modern cats have managed to maintain some of their heritage – hunting and stuff – whilst prostituting their affections in return for food and shelter. Cat's are having their fishcake and eating it. It must take incredible effort of genetic will to keep those traditions alive down through the generations. As much as I detest the species, I admire that resolve. Reluctantly, I have to admit they're my role models. Like them, I want my descendants to have food and shelter provided, but with the freedom of expression that cats retain. In fact, I want my offspring's status and domestication / tradition balance to be better than that of the pussies – and that's no pipe dream. The biggest mistake most wild animals are making right now is believing the opportunities to become kept livestock have bolted and that the stable door has been locked shut. The door is never closed on evolution. It's never too late to change. All it takes is that first positive move. If you could look back through time at the development of any species, at some point you'd find an individual who made a move, for some reason, in a new direction. If there's one thing you can definitely say about evolution, it's that it's constantly changing. Evolution is like a world champion boxer – it doesn't stand still for a moment. I am such a champion. A prize rat. So I am making that move.

In the future, when they study the successful and popular species of domesticated rat 'Rattus modernus' they'll find me at the vanguard. I am going to spawn a whole new species of rat. I want my descendants to have better prospects than my con-temporaries could even imagine. I want a slice of the domesticated pie for my offspring. If you have young of your own, you'll know that providing for your children makes you feel proud. If you know that your endeavours have secured a positive future for your grandchildren too, you're prouder still. Imagine then, the sense of pride at knowing that you've provided specific advantage for a whole new species – all of whom are ultimately the fruits of your loins.

I'm a big lad. That's important. My studies have revealed that you need to achieve a certain size before humans are willing to let you join the 'empowered domesticated' category. Too small, and they'll stick you in a cage. That's not a mutually beneficial domesticated relationship. Too big, and you'll have to live in a field or a barn; spending your working life carrying or pulling some human's burden before being forcibly retired and fed to the dogs. Large animals are, by very nature of their physicality, excluded from the inner sanctum – the home. Things are going well with my plan so far. I'm a good size. My large-dimension gene has been picked-up by many of my children. In the right environment, with high-protein nutrition, future generations will get even bigger. Within a few selectively channelled generations, my babies could grow bigger than the average cat or ridiculous lap dog. That would really help on the status front.

That's enough theorising for a while. Let's get down to business. I'm big and I live with a big bloke. To be honest, but slightly disloyal; he's fat. Huge. Dangerously obese. On top of that, he's lazy as hell and his standard of hygiene is shocking. And he doesn't have a single human friend. But, like everyone, he likes company. He wants to be loved. All these traits are ideal for the success of my plan. That's why I selected him. No one is going to come round and pry and interfere. This means we can get on with our development whilst he benefits from letting us do so. He inherited our house – so he's here till he dies. He lives off fast food, which he spills everywhere and never clears-up. The house is in a shocking state of repair, so there are holes everywhere that provide access for my extended family. He also gets love from us. We take it in turns to curl up on his voluminous thighs, creating temporary cotton-covered flesh-craters while he strokes us. The fat git is perfect. We practically worship him. We call him Titan. Stage one of my evolutionary plan was finding him. Stage two is establishing the template inter-species relationship with him here in this house. Stage three is both practical – enlargening our habitats; and promotional – creating the right conditions for our expanding movement. In stage three we move on. That's when my offspring will become exposed to the wider human population. This phase demands finding more fat losers or similarly pathetic specimens whose lives we can add value to. We will spread out across the globe; four-legged founding fathers, following the footsteps of human pioneers of times past. And as the momentum of our movement builds; as more people become aware of us, we'll need to generate some damned good PR. We need that to shake off the bad press we've attracted in recent centuries. PR will make or break you in this modern age. To gain positive, media-grabbing exposure, you need an angle. Early dogs were 'Hunting Companions' and 'Security Guards'. They helped with the hunting and guarded the dwellings. Cats were 'Rodent Suppressors' – promising to keep me and my brothers under control, the bastards. But neither species, because they made their moves thousands of years ago, is suited to dealing with the major problems of the modern human habitat – organic waste and bugs. We are. Although we may have come late to the domestication game, we now have a huge advantage – we are the animal best equipped to deal with these modern challenges. And if we can do it well enough, we will be the beasts of the moment and humans will abandon their historical allies in favour of us – Rattus modernus.

No human wants bugs in their houses. They want to live in close-to sterile environments. Cockroaches, ants, woodlice and spiders are the new pariahs, the new parasites, the new predators. Pesticides are expensive, temporary and increasingly regarded as non-environmentally friendly. Humans want green solutions to everything. And what could be more eco-friendly than a naturally adapted animal sorting out their problems for them? And we're not just ideally profiled for environmental sustainability – we're thorough. It's in our nature to investigate every nook and cranny. We'll have the hidden corners so well covered that they'll never need to get down on their knees and scrub again. Whilst our particular host may be exceptionally lazy and slobfully disinclined to sort out his own mess, he's not radically different to the rest of his worldwide colony. His whole species is obsessed with labour-saving. Give them a way of not doing something they weren't that troubled about not doing in the first place, and they'll happily commit wholeheartedly to not doing it ever again.

My family and I eat Titan's bugs. He's probably one of the most unhygienic humans on the planet, but he's got less bugs in his house than the most pristine of hospital wards. On top of that, we get rid of organic waste too. Every morsel of food that escapes his guzzling gob is consumed by my many offspring. We remove every crumb of food from his take-away food containers – we even eat the bones. We lick clean his toilet bowl , which needs doing daily. There's not a spot of organic matter on the pots or crockery in his kitchen. We even eat the toilet tissues he throws onto his bedroom floor.

Whilst looking after Titan properly generates plenty of work, I've set a rule that no more than one hundred of us should be in the house at any one time. I don't want him to worry that we might be overrunning the place. He needs to feel that no more than the required workforce is sheltering under his roof. The first rule of domestication is to make the human think they're doing you a favour. Humans have sensitive egos. Pump them up and they'll love you, dent them and they'll reject you. Maintaining the hundred rule has given us a whole new social order. We have Gate Guards counting rats in and out. There are Messengers to keep the lines of communication open between Gate Guards in various locations. There are Inspectors and Heads of Working Parties. Then, on top of the permanent designations, such as those just mentioned, there are many part time roles briefed-in to the general populace on an 'as needed' basis. These functions include designated Storers, Nest-Builders, Track Maintenance Teams – that kind of thing. We even have a police force. In reality, these are quickly-assembled lynch-mobs made up of the toughest individuals. Whilst this is slightly rough and ready approach, it's early days for our developing culture. Things will get more refined as the genetically improved generations succeed one another like upgraded home computers. I think you get the picture. We are a new generation of rats – coordinated, and future-facing. We're focused. We're house-trained. We're thorough. We're interactive and affectionate. We eat bugs. We eat organic waste. We've got Titan's place running shipshape. I love the irony of that expression; we've boarded and turned around the stinking, sinking ship that was once his pigsty of a home.

The status quo won't last forever. One day, Titan is going to die. With the kind of rubbish he tucks away, a heart-attack can't be too far off in human years. That's when phase two will come to an end and phase three kicks in. Personally, I'd love nothing more than to witness it myself. But, with our life expectancy as low as it is at the moment, I'll probably be long gone by then. However, I'm a realist and I've anticipated that eventuality. Plans for the next phase, therefore, are already drawn-up. I have instructed that Titan going man-tits-up is my lot's cue to move on. By the time he snuffs it there will be thousands of us – most living out in the sewer pipe, admittedly. The order when this happens is to split into as many sustainable groups as possible. Each group will need to contain sufficient representatives of all the leading disciplines. These self-contained pioneer communities are charged with heading onward and outward to new frontiers and finding suitable replacement hosts. We can't and won't hang around at Titan's lair for congratulations. Human medical teams and house clearance specialists wouldn't immediately understand our role. Those two groups are notoriously anti-rat. We need to be well clear of the site before they arrive. Forensic scientists will be our heralds. They will be perplexed with the contrast between clear signs of the disgusting state of Titan's lifestyle and the impeccable condition of his home. Faced with this conundrum, they'll be professionally inquisitive. They'll investigate. They'll weigh up the evidence and anecdotal tales, and they'll put two and two together. However unlikely it might be, the only possible solution they'll come up with, is us, Rattus modernus. They'll smell, and detect, a rat. Even if they try to suppress it, news will slowly leak out of their extraordinary discovery. By that time we'll be serving other clients. The future discovery of further successful projects will fortify and enhance our new reputation. We'll proliferate, and our stature will grow with each positive story. Word of us will eventually spread from urban myth into accepted reality. By the time humans are ready to accept the services of my selectively evolved descendants as partners against grime, we'll be everywhere, sorting out the chaotic world and bug infestations of hundreds of once-squalid human habitats. The last step to complete will be the small leap from supporting marginal lifestyles to being at the very heart of the mainstream.

That's another moment I'd love to witness – the point at which we're no longer scampering around in the shadows as an underground movement. We will become the must-have. We will be deemed the most successful example of domestication ever – or, as I prefer to call it, 'Human-Slash-Non-Human-Interdependability'. I'll be ancient history by then. But my genome will live on. I will be the father of a great new species. Modern rats and humans will flourish alongside one another. We will become a vital part of a new and long-lasting human epoch. Looking further forward into the future, to the time when they eventually wipe themselves out, I can't see a reason why we can't become the new masters of the planet. We'll have the organisation, the numbers and the know-how, to inherit the earth. If my initial plan works out, it'll demonstrate that we've got the potential to rapidly respond to changing circumstances – and that we could evolve again. If one of my descendants inherits my ability to combine incredible insight with strong leadership, he could initiate the next progression and lead us on to seek out the next gap in the market. Inside a million years, we could become Rattus erectus. My descendants could eventually sit at the top of the food chain. And if we do end up running this joint one day, rather than scurrying across it, Rattus erectus will trace back their genetic inheritance to find me – the originator of all their success. They will write books about me, make films about me, they might even build temples to me. I will be named the greatest visionary of all time, the original instigator of our species' triumph. I will be their Grandfather, their benevolent über-ancestor, their God. But right now, the fat git's just wanked into a snotty tissue and chucked in on the floor. Time to do my duty and start gobbling.

HELL BREAKS

The Devil is offering holidays in Hell. They're proving to be quite popular. Mortal souls are enjoying all that Hell has to offer. Lucifer's got an ulterior motive, of course. For the last several millennia he's relied on 'worldly goods' gift packages to keep recruitment numbers up; temptation deals where you get mortal benefits in return for immortal commitment. Those deals, combined with a generally high level of degenerate behaviour, kept Hell pretty full in the past. Unfortunately for the poor Embodiment Of Evil, the age of mass communication seriously screwed things up. It began to go wrong for him when we started mass-producing books. Word started to get round that behaving badly could cost you big-style in the long run. Admittedly, megalomaniac moralisers have been trying to influence the masses since ancient times. Early priests and playwrights arranged festivals and theatrical shows that warned of the dangers of doing things like killing our fathers or shagging our mothers. But ordinary folk only got to see a play or a religious festival once every two or three years. That wasn't sufficient exposure to virtuous concepts to really get inside their minds. Shows were remembered for their spectacle, rather than their substance.

As civilisation advanced and the monotheistic religions took over, they preached stricter control of public behaviour. The custodians of their messages tried to make us obedient and well behaved. But priests and monks invariably preached one thing and did another. Religious leaders were just another aristocracy – staring at us through the stained glass of cathedrals and monasteries rather than the arrow slits of castles and watchtowers. The moment the masses felt safe from the prying eyes of their irreverent ecclesiastical overlords, they just got on with what they wanted to do anyway. Morality was skin-deep everywhere, and recruitment wasn't a problem for Satan.

Widespread literacy changed the landscape. Books that warned of the dangers of selling out to the devil, infiltrated ordinary homes, bringing moral thinking into the heart of common folk's private shelters. And it wasn't just religious tomes that banged-on about the benefits of making righteous decisions. For some reason, rising literacy went hand in hand with rising moral standards; with even secular scribes choosing to encourage human goodness. Do your research and you'll discover that pretty much every piece of poetry or prose promotes wholesomeness – either by praising the virtuous or condemning the cruel. So, even without the divine assistance of a coordinated campaign to encourage goodwill on earth, moral works soon reigned supreme from their privileged positions on our mantelpieces and bookshelves. Hot on the heels of mass-produced moralising literature came broadcast media. Radios, then television sets, compounded the bombardment of do-good messages. Pretty much every household in the modern world was being regularly invaded with electromagnetic moralistic material. Although we are free to choose what entertainment we consume, let's face it: how many radio shows, movies or television programmes celebrate the greatness of evil? Modern media formats may have brought a revolution in home entertainment, but they've stuck with the age-old moral fibre of their page-bound predecessors. Boil most audio-visual entertainment down to its bare bones, and you'll see that decent behaviour is being presented as the de facto default guideline for human interaction. Baddies generally get their comeuppance and goodies are generally celebrated for their efforts, even if that has to happen posthumously. When did you last watch a documentary celebrating the joys of coveting, the satisfaction of gluttony or the thrill and profitability of theft? In addition to the irresistible tidal wave of high-minded creativity, The Prince of Darkness has been specifically rumbled by some very astute writers. They've challenged the logic of his original recruitment policy. The ploy of offering worldly gifts in return for eternal condemnation to Hell has been steadily undermined from Faust through Angel Heart to The Devil's Advocate (starring Keanu Reeves).

Confronted with a mass tendency towards decency, the Devil needed a new strategy. He found inspiration from the dolly birds who offer out free samples at train stations and in night clubs. And drug dealers. He saw that we're suckers for free samples. It took capitalism in all its glory to reveal the power of giving away a little something-for-nothing in order to get people hooked. Our desire to try something before we commit and our love of freebies was a potent enough brew in itself – but add that to our current spoiled demand for new and interesting holiday destinations and you have an irresistible concoction. The Devil saw that sampler holidays in Hell might not be such a bad idea. He set himself an initial three-month trial period and hasn't looked back since.

There are several different types of vacation on offer: there are traditional two week family holidays in chalet-based resorts along the River Styx; there are weekend breaks in various Hellish cities for busy professionals; and there are the very popular lava-lake cruises – mostly taken-up by the senior end of the age demographic. I'll explain some of the benefits of those destinations.

The River Styx runs along the border of Hell. It sustains no life whatsoever. The common misconception is that the Styx runs black and fetid. Devoid of plant and animal life, the water is in fact crystal clear. With the water lacking nasties like sharks or stinging jellyfish, you know your children will be safe swimming in it. At the heart of Hell is a furnace that burns 24/7. It's been burning 24/7 since the universe was created. Up close, it's intentionally unbearable. But at the coastal edges of Satan's domain, the heat is comparable to the South Coast of Spain in late August/ early September – without the sun's harmful UVA and UVB rays. As for the local inhabitants; the more tortured a soul is set to be, the deeper in Hell they're sent. The very centre of Hell is reserved for the most damned spirits of most evil humans to have ever breathed. These supremely wicked individuals attract the most abhorrent demons imaginable; tasked with delivering everlasting unbearable punishment. At the edges things are much nicer. Around the riverside resorts, you get a better a better class of demon and pretty mild sinners. During a typical two-week family break near the coast, you might not witness a single act of demonic retribution. All in all, it's a great location for families.

Then there are city breaks in Hell. If you can handle the more malevolent elements, they totally outclass worldly urban trips. Hellish cities boast awesome architectural features that predate the earliest human civilisations. In addition to the stunning buildings, there are gastronomic creations that will excite the palate of the most demanding diner – with innumerable cooking traditions utilising all the ingredients that have ever existed in the universe. And if it's entertainment you're after, there are all manners of live shows, featuring entities and performances that it would take way too long to describe, but I can tell you this; if you like to party, you'll never party like a mortal soul in Hell. With all this and so much more to offer, city breaks in Hell never fail to stimulate even the most world-weary traveller.

Alternatively, if you're looking for something a little more relaxing, there are gentle cruises around the geological wonders of Hell's lava lakes. As I mentioned earlier, these attract the more serene crowd, those not seeking bright lights or frantic activity – and they are made to feel at home. On the liners, you are isolated from the everyday business of Hell. You won't be exposed to the torture of a single soul. The ships are staffed entirely by demons who have retired from the gruelling business of punishing sinners. These superannuated servants of Satan have turned their backs on the business of dishing-out nastiness and are incredibly civil and charming. And, because they know many of their passengers will soon be suffering at the hands of their younger, less jaded relatives, they take it upon themselves to coach the elderly in readiness for eternal damnation. This additional unadvertised service has become extremely popular through word of mouth and provides extra incentive for the purple rinse brigade and their white-moustachioed husbands.

These are just three examples – so, with such a range of unforgettable breaks on offer, it's hardly surprising that holidays in Hell have become immensely popular. What *has* surprised me is the supplementary effect these free trips have had on human behaviour. The Devil's gamble, you'd have to say, has paid-off. I'd forgive you for thinking that seeing Hell first-hand might encourage more people to live virtuous lives. The opposite is true. More souls than ever are heading to Hell after Judgement. Familiarity it seems, breeds contentment not contempt. Although tourists know there are dark parts of Hell that remain hidden from prying eyes, they have grown accustomed to the Hellish ways of life they are exposed to. The Hell section is now the biggest by far of any of the travel sections in bookshops (religious ones apart). And our ease with Hell as a vacation destination has made us feel more comfortable with the thought of it being our final destination. It has encouraged more of us to sin a little – since we are less worried about the prospect of eventually being sent there. Put simply, you can have more fun on Earth and afterwards have good times in Hell. It's the best of both worlds.

Before Hell opened up its gates to holiday makers, the difference between Heaven and Hell was presented as a simple choice between infinite joy or eternal, unbearable damnation. That apparent Hobson's choice encouraged many of us to live thoroughly decent lives. A peek at life in Hell has shown us that things aren't quite so black and white. Of course, holidaymakers are very aware that they are just tourists, and they can see for themselves that all the souls in Hell suffer some level of discomfort. But some condemned souls have it far worse than others. Hell is an anti-meritocracy. If you've only been minor league bad, your eternity in Hell might end up meaning you're trapped in a rather fascinating, vibrant city experiencing some light torturing every third week or so. And whilst you're being flayed by a demon, you could be staring at breathtaking scenery. To the casual observer, eternal damnation for the vast majority of Hell's citizens doesn't look so bad. It's just a case of judging how bad you can get away with being during your mortal phase. Of course we're talking about the grey areas of sin here – those amongst us destined for the most terrible districts of Hades are going there regardless of any recruitment drives by Lucifer. He's never needed to incentivise the inherently evil. Really bad people have always disappeared into the depths of Hell, and they always will. Where the Devil was losing recruits was amongst the minor transgressors – and since free breaks to the Underworld were introduced, those numbers are well up. And because this mildly devilish demographic accounts for the majority of the human population, the long-fought battle between good and evil is going Satan's way. Heaven can't, or won't, fight back. Angels claim Paradise is a place of absolute and eternal joy. They protest that you can't, by definition, sample a little bit of Heaven – you can't have a weekend break there. Well, their 'Holier than Thou' attitude is costing them dearly, as their moral high-ground is becoming more desolate by the day. And whilst I don't profess to be an authority on these matters, even I can see that the pure of spirit are losing the numbers game. Perhaps it's time for them to swallow their outdated principles and take a leaf out of Lucifer's book.

WHAT A FIX!

Ned and Joy were inseparable. Literally. They were in love from the moment they saw one another. At the time of their first meeting, they both had different partners. Ned was seeing a striking and statuesque waitress from Denmark. Joy was seeing a professional athlete. They both seemed wonderfully happy with their respective matches. Cupid had other plans.

They first met when they went to an after-show party with their respective partners. The party followed the premier of a wonderful romantic play. Both couples knew cast members. Different cast members. The party was a glamorous affair attended by cohorts of beautiful people. Ned and Joy mixed in glitzy circles and were used to being around wonderful human specimens of both genders (it is important for you to know that both of them were regularly exposed to glorious human forms, and that they didn't fall in love purely out of physical attraction). The nature of the show may have affected them; heightened their intellectual and emotional desire for an incredible intimate relationship – but being in that state was unusual for neither of them. The particular circumstances of that night were not sufficient to cement their love. One can only say that Ned and Joy were destined to be united, because the instant their glances collided, Destiny drove felt, but unseen, multi-pointed hooks into their hearts and those barbs were tethered with a single strand of invisible, unseverable twine... I apologise, but I must interrupt the tale for moment here. The concept of destiny deeply troubles me. If our lives are predestined, this negates the value of us living them. Because of this, I use the word destined with great reserve. In this tale, I use it to mean that the force drawing them together was so powerful and inescapable, that you can only conclude that from the moment they met, they were meant to be together. In this sense, 'destined' does not mean 'pre-determined'; it means 'inevitable with the insight of hindsight'. There are a trillion things that could have prevented them from ever meeting. But they did meet. And from the moment they first bathed mentally undressed in one another's lustful stares, they'd captured one another's hearts. From then on, they were destined to be together.

How they engineered the break-ups of their existing relationships and beat a path to one another's lives is unimportant. Within a short period of time, they were seeing each other. At the start of their relationship, whilst slightly smothered by fresh leaves that had fallen from the shaken trees of their previous relationships, their passion smouldered unseen. During this period they maintained their existing lifestyles. But the fire picked-up very quickly and flames began to replace the revealing wisps of smoke that curled silently away from them. They became a small bonfire in the undergrowth which rapidly grew into a raging wild fire. Once that had taken hold, they fuelled and consumed themselves, then fuelled and consumed themselves again, like a blazing forest that magically regenerates, never running out of combustible material. Others were less poetic in their assessment of Ned and Joy's conduct. They saw the billowing smoke, but deemed it something foul, like noxious fumes emanating from burning crack cocaine. To those observers, Ned and Joy were all-consumed addicts, abandoning social graces and devoting themselves slavishly to their privately-shared narcotic. When they were apart, they yearned for one another's company. When they were together, they behaved like sex-obsessed teenagers, utterly absorbed in each other, as if tasting erotic interaction for the very first time. Friends found their behaviour hard to deal with. Their professional and social lives suffered immensely. Even family members were uncomfortable with their constant need for one another. As a couple, they soon didn't fit in anywhere. They were rejected. Junkies don't mind being rejected. Addiction is a vicious circle. All you want is your drug, so you lose interest in anything else. Those around you cannot cope with your addiction and eventually they leave you to get on with it. Being deserted by friends and family, and sacked from their jobs, did not worry Ned and Joy. In fact, being presented with huge amounts of uninterrupted time together was exactly what they desired. Their old lives went up in smoke. Once there were no remaining ties, they sold-up, and left the city they'd lived in. They decided they wanted a simple life where they could share everything; every experience, every taste, sound and smell. They downsized and bought a small farm in the mountains. It was a goat-and-arable-farm of a decent size. It had a good herd of healthy animals and easily sustained them. It cost a lot less than their place in the city, so they had money left over too. They felt set-up for life.

Ned and Joy loved their new existence. The nearest human habitation was over six miles away. Travellers rarely trekked past. They produced wonderful cheese, which a travelling gourmet food tradesman collected once a month before swiftly going on his way. They had their own fresh water spring which gurgled out refreshing healthy natural spring water. The herd, as is the nature of goats, needed very little looking after. On the rare occasions they needed to visit it, the walk to the town was picturesque and secluded – offering plenty of good fucking locations en route. Quite simply, they could spend hours every day having passionate sex with one another. Which is what they did. They consummated their relationship constantly.

If you ever met them, you'd say their minds were linked. They were like one person. They desired the same things; they shared memories like they had experienced them from a singular perspective; they enjoyed the same food, in the same way; they even breathed in sync (whether sat pawing one another or looking at each other longingly from opposite sides of a room). They were as intertwined as two spirits could be and they matched their spiritual interdependence with constant physical interconnection. Ned and Joy were the most into-each-other couple in the history of humanity. But the tale of their relationship eclipses romance. Theirs was a love affair so intense it led to fusion.

One seemingly unremarkable morning, soon after Ned had returned from his daily inspection of the herd and Joy had laid breakfast, they were shagging as usual. They waltzed naked around the kitchen table in an erotic dance of physical union. They bumped into, and copulated against or on top of, every piece of furniture they encountered during their rousing duet. As always, objects and foodstuffs that came to hand were used as sex aids and stimuli. They fucked and fucked and fucked and fucked and fucked. Up to this point, things were relatively routine. When they both eventually came together, they were lying on the large draining board beside the sink. They stayed pressed together through to the very last squeeze of Ned's sperm into Joy's vagina.

After that, they lay together some more as Joy ground her pussy around his still-firm cock, coming one more time. Then they lay together some more in post-orgasmic abandon. They lay there until thirst and hunger cruelly forced them to disengage. At this point things got a little weird. When they began to unravel themselves from their lengthy post-coital embrace, they found that they couldn't. Well, not fully. During the last phase of their love-making, Joy's left hand and Ned's right hand had been clasped together. They stayed that way. The skin of their palms and the insides of their fingers had become one. Where they touched, the cells of the skin on their hands had joined together as tightly as the atoms of a diamond. The connection ran to the root of the cell structures, with not only their epidermis, but also their dermis, combining to form a singular mass of living tissue.

This strange physical bonding surprised them. But it didn't trouble them. They got on with their lives as best they could, redesigning their garments, altering the way they carried out their regular tasks, but still fucking lots. Although Ned and Joy had pretty much kept themselves to themselves since moving to the mountains, they weren't completely isolated from society. They made their occasional shag-laced journeys into town; there was the cheese trader and a few others who visited them from time to time and there were occasional passers-by. Word got out. People started talking about a couple who were permanently stuck together (it was already widely known and discussed that they copulated constantly). They started to get visitors. Inquisitive folk would hike all the way to their home to stare at them. At first the cemented couple tried to hide from their onlookers. But trying to evade the gazes prolonged each onlooker's stay. They'd hang around until they'd had a good eyeful. So Ned and Joy gave them a good look and eventually got used to the visitors. Rumours of the connection were confirmed by first-hand witnesses. The trickle of spectators became a steady flow, which resulted in a constant band of onlookers milling about, so they let the local authority build a hiking lodge in their grounds. It got very cold in the mountains. Travellers would spend a few awe-struck nights in it before moving on. Allowing the construction of the shelter was typical of this warm-hearted couple's generosity.

Over time, the nature of the pilgrims changed. For the first few months it was casual voyeurs, living relatively close by or in the area on holiday, who made the trek. But after the initial surge of general fascination died down, those prepared to make the arduous, meandering journey were increasingly individuals with a healthy / unhealthy interest in human sexual activity. Soon Ned and Joy's visitors were almost entirely composed of those obsessed with, dedicated to, or addicted to sex, many of whom made repeated and prolonged visits to their little fertile plateau. Their followers included people with sexual commitment or performance issues; those engaged in sex or eroticism as a profession; and those with a scientific or academic interest in rutting. In the lodge, groups of 'devotees' regularly engaged in impromptu orgies and sex shows. Ned and Joy knew what was going on, but never partook, they were only ever interested in one another. They were as compassionate as they were passionate, and always made time for their disciples. They gave talks on sexual matters and the small fees they requested in return compensated them to some extent for the inconvenience of their unique physical connection. Which seemed fair. Ned and Joy became sages for the sex-needy. But whenever they weren't busy preaching or otherwise tending to their disparate flock, they got on with their fucking.

One day, during a particularly good shag, with both sets of hands clasped together (the stuck set on one side and the previously detachable set on the other), the phenomena repeated itself. Ned's left hand and Joy's right became affixed. Having one hand permanently stuck to one of your lover's can be an inconvenience. Having both sets of hands permanently attached can be a downright nuisance. From this point on, the lovers needed constant attendance. Fortunately, their already substantial throng of worshippers grew. There are innumerable reasons why many more people would choose to see them once they were joined at both hands, but this tale is long enough without me listing them. In essence, the reoccurrence of the event hugely enhanced their credibility as the living embodiment; the manifested deity of human sexual attraction. Added to that, their increased vulnerability elicited a hugely amplified duty of care from their disciples. The lodge was extended. Pilgrims were attracted from all around the world. The conjoined pair were tended to day and night. A global business sprang up, trading on their condition and lectures. Ned and Joy, at one time vilified for their sexual obsession, became internationally celebrated for it. Even old friends and family came to see them – they were too wrapped in one another to waste time bearing grudges, and welcomed their pre-physical fixation companions with open arms (metaphorically speaking). The assembled masses treated their close associates like members of a royal family. A royal fuck family.

The next development in our couple's physiology isn't too hard to imagine. They became intimately joined. This isn't without precedent in the natural world. It happens with foxes when they shag. The dog fox's cock gets trapped in the vixen's vagina. It can take hours of painful yelping before the vixen's tunnel relaxes enough for the dog to escape with his manhood. The purpose behind this is for every drip of sperm to be securely deposited within the foxy fox hole. With Ned and Joy, the condition was permanent. The outer skin of his penis became welded to her vaginal wall. Separation was impossible. You might think that this spelt the end for our loving couple. It didn't. They could still do everything they needed to do to stay alive. There was enough of a gap in the intimate conjunction for Ned's urine, and other bodily fluids, to pass. They coped easily with that. After all, they'd been shitting and pissing in front of (and on) each other since way before even their first pair of hands became fused. Their lives, and their sexual ardour, didn't dissipate. Their celebrity grew, all their needs were attended to, and they spent every moment welded together. Weird as their predicament was, they were very happy.

A problem did arise, however. On the night Ned and Joy became genitally fused, they conceived. I've no idea why it took such a long time, and so much intercourse, but that's when it happened. Over the next nine and a bit months, their baby grew between them. Specialist medical staff had to be drafted in to attend to their, and their baby's, developing needs. As Joy's belly swelled, life became increasingly more difficult for them both. Ned's back arched backwards painfully, and the pressure from both without and within became horribly difficult for Joy to bear. For the last three months of the gestation, the tightly fastened pair were extremely difficult to move. They developed bed sores and their health suffered generally. On top of their declining well being, they were traumatised by the impending birth itself. They tried to come to terms with the frightening prospect of how that would happen. The traditional route was – quite obviously – blocked.

Caesarean was the only other option. Ned's body position made that very difficult, but there were no other possibilities.

The day came, and the stuck couple's considerable wealth had paid for the best experts in the field. During the procedure, it was planned that Ned would be held to the right side of Joy to enable the lead surgeon to gain access to Joy's womb through the left side of her abdomen. The anaesthetist advised, due to the complicated nature of the procedure, that both parties be given a general anaesthetic. They both refused citing the fact that since they had been through everything together, including experiences beyond our ability to imagine, they would not be found wanting on this occasion. They would not let anaesthesia deprive them of the opportunity to witness the greatest event of their lives so far. Joy sensibly opted for an epidural. Ned was already on strong pain killers for his twisted back, and felt they would be sufficient. Everything seemed in place. A special operating theatre had been built next to Ned and Joy's home. The exhausted couple were wheeled in and lifted, Ned uppermost, onto the private operating table. The lead surgeon gave the nod, and several strong young doctors gently manoeuvred Ned to the side of his beloved's swollen belly. The first confident incision was quickly made. It was at this point that the medical team's meticulous plan rapidly unravelled.

Ned and joy, it turned out, were joined to one another by more than skin. The nervous systems in their hands and genitals had connected too. Over time, where they were joined, their nerve networks had made their desire to share one another's experiences a reality. Their unquenchable passion somehow drew their neural conduits together. The branch-like sensory-message carrying systems pushed outwards through their conjoined skin like seedlings slowly working their way through parking-lot concrete. When, like climbing plants, their nervous reaching feelers met, they merged to form an interconnected grid like the singular nerve network of certain types of mated angler fish. It has been argued that the DNA-deep desire of their nerve networks to link up, is what first caused the cohesion of their flesh. Their ardour was so intense that together they physically manifested the ability to share senses. During sex, they not only enjoyed fucking, but also sharing in the mutual experience of being fucked. They were as close as two previously separated human forms could ever be.

When the surgeon cut through several layers of Joy's abdomen, she felt nothing. The epidural blocked all the pain below the point in her spine where the anaesthetist had driven his needle. Ned felt the cut. Intensely. The surgeon may as well have been cutting though Ned's raw belly with a vinegar-marinated razor-sharp kitchen knife. The searing pain of someone slicing through layers of living tissue sent him into convulsions. His uncontrollable flailing body sprang round to cover Joy's stomach, trapping the surgeon's hand. The surgeon instinctively withdrew his hand, maintaining a tight professional grasp of the scalpel. The ultra-sharp blade cut a further, unplanned furrow across Joy's belly. She began to bleed profusely. Ned's spasms became even more violent. The situation was critical. Instant action was needed. Ned, in agony but lucid, did what any future father, devoted lover and honourable man would do. He ordered the anaesthetist to knock him out. The situation was so desperate that an anaesthetic would not have acted quickly enough. So the anaesthetist, an ex Olympic rower, whacked him in the temple with a heavy piece of hospital equipment. Ned was rendered instantly unconscious. His limp body was pulled to one side, and the flustered surgeon hurriedly removed the infant.

Joy and Ned both died within the hour. Joy gushed life from her savage, unstemmable wounds. Ned died of a brain haemorrhage without regaining consciousness. (Although their anaesthetist was incredibly experienced in the art of rendering patients unconscious, the art of using brutal blows to the skull with solid objects in order to do so, is still a relatively hit and miss operation.) The authorities took care of their son. They named him Fusion. He is now thirty-seven years old and has renamed himself Dave. He plays computer games all the time. And he's a virgin.

DAMSON JAM

Met God's ex-wife once.

She was wearing a size eighteen, big-print floral dress, like my Nan used to wear, and selling home-made jam at a church fête.

They called her Edith.

I said to her, "don't I recognise you?"

She told me she got that all the time.

It was her break, so we had tea together, next to the lucky dip.

She regretted the break-up, but said he was impossible to live with.

I understood. I was recovering from a failed relationship myself.

She said she enjoyed having more time to herself, spending much of it in the garden. Called it her own little corner of paradise. That's where all the fruit for her preserves comes from.

I bought a jar of damson.

It tasted like ten thousand tonnes of fruit had been squashed into each spoonful.

After a night out, friends would always crash at my house. In the morning there'd be one request; toast with damson jam.

I'd spread it so thinly you could hardly see its treacle-purple tones. But even rationed ultra-sparingly, there was enough flavour to set taste buds fizzing like Bonfire Night sparklers.

But, like a celebrated prophet, the jam's popularity hastened its own demise. It was consumed by the converts and I was left with a cylindrical monument to its former glory.

An empty tomb.

The jar.

These days, every weekend, I drive obsessively up and down the country, bouncing from fête to fête, bazaar to bazaar, hoping to find Edith and her jams again. Weekdays I plan my route, aiming to take-in at least five events where local produce will be on sale.

There are worse obsessions.

When I'm not planning, I fantasise about what jams I might buy if I find her again. Would something obvious like strawberry bring the greatest surprise – the mundane transformed into the marvellous? Perhaps gooseberry, already a zingy preserve, would be more even more excruciatingly delicious than her regular offerings? Or would an unusual choice, something like quince jelly, prove the most magical of all her creations?

Of course, if I find Edith, I'll buy-up all her stock. And I'll get her address, and her itinerary for the next fifty years.

In the meantime, I wonder one thing. Could her ex, divine and magnificent as he is, produce such extraordinarily wonderful jams?

IMMORTAL

If you're lucky enough to own a piece of land, whether it's just enough for two folding chairs and a wine bottle, or expansive enough for herds of buffalo, there's one thing I can guarantee you: things will happen in your corner of the Earth about which you'll never know anything. Land is like time – it holds many secrets.

Our land comprised twelve acres of mainly pasture – that's enough real estate to keep a dozen or so cattle, a couple of ponies, a dog and a handful of cats. Which is what we kept. At the centre, the heart of the territory, was our home; a centuries-old stone cottage. It had grown, like a hollow granite cancer, in spits and spats, since the foundation rock was laid. When it was still small, it was one of several stone cottages that once formed a thriving hamlet. For a reason I'll reveal later; although the rest withered, ours grew. Evidence of the hamlet's former glory were easy to find. The remains of two other dwellings, ravaged by neglect, stood in our fields. Further multi-cell stone outlines could be found under leaf mould in the woods beyond the pasture. All were remnants of once-cherished man-made growths, rendered useless by the neutralisation of their human nuclei. In themselves, these earth-covered granite floor plans are nothing particularly special – the world is tattooed all over with the markings of lost micro and macro civilisations. But there's more to this tale than archaeology.

Every hundred years or so, someone on this planet doesn't die when they should. They get to a certain age, then stop ageing. Our immortal is one of them. He lives under the remains of the cottage in the North Field. That ruin is distinctively, noticeably, different to all the rest. It stands out. There is a lot more left of it than the cottages in the East Field, the West Field, or amongst the trees beyond. When we lived on the farm, his cottage still had four impressive walls, three of which were almost complete along their lengths, standing their full height of seven feet. The dwellings in the other two fields, once equal in stature, had shrivelled to buried stumps – grass covered mounds indicating where proud walls once stood. They looked liked elongated grave mounds concealing a past they were ashamed of.

The cottage in the North Field had been the Immortal's home before he retreated to subterranean security. If he'd lived a normal life span, it would be in the same state of disrepair as the rest of the relics. For a while, he thought that if he kept himself to himself, he'd be able to carry on residing there. He did so, living in it well into his hundred and thirties. Up to the point he abandoned it, he'd spent those thirteen decades (except for periods during the occasional foreign war or two) sheltering between its four walls. But he was deluded thinking that the simple country folk would let him carry on forever, and local prejudice eventually drove him underground. Resist the ageing process for a decade or two, and people think you're lucky. Resist it for a generation longer, and they start to think you're evil incarnate. As The Immortal refused to grow old, spooked, jealous mortals grew first restless, then aggressive. Under assault from all sides, like a First

World War shell dodger, or a Vietcong fighter with an aversion to napalm, he dug in.

He now lives in a bunker, underneath his old home. He didn't relocate – or 'run off'; as he always described that option to me. He stayed where his home was, because when all his friends and family had died, all he had left was where he was from. His geographic identity is the lifebelt he's clung to through subsequent ever-shifting tides of humanity. Initially, although he no longer lived inside, out of pride and loyalty, he kept the old house in perfect order. It took considerable effort to do so – to stop it from falling apart without being caught. He had to work at night like a miserable thief – which he resented. But even that surreptitious mission had to be abandoned when, a century or so after he'd retreated underground, he finally accepted the pristine condition of his residence was fuelling rumours of his continued existence. He was creating anti-camouflage with an empty dwelling that refused to fall into disrepair. If he was found out, he'd be forced to leave the land he loves. So, with echoes of his presence inspiring local legends, eventually, reluctantly, he allowed his precious abode begin slowly crumbling above him. He switched from a policy of repairing every bit of damage to just repairing some; slowing down rather than holding-back the ravages of time. Even part-deserting the home he was born and raised in, hurt. A lot. It was the last time he let anything upset him; and that was nearly two hundred years ago.

Immortals aren't invincible, by the way. They can feel physical pain. Cut them and they bleed, bash them and they bruise. They just don't age. When they get injured, they repair more quickly than us – though, like us, it takes them longer to overcome bigger injuries. The Marvel character Wolverine is actually based on a real immortal. The Immortal has no idea whether or not he could be killed. For all he knows, he might actually die if he suffered a serious enough injury. In fact, he's wished for one many times; even contemplated suicidal actions. The only thing that prevents him from attempting to take his own life is the fear that he'd continue to exist but be permanently incapacitated. If the curse of eternal life wasn't bad enough, imagine enduring it in a state of total paralysis. He wonders what that would be like; lying alive, undecaying, undiscovered as fresh soil slowly creeps over him, like it has over the stunted ruins of the cottages. Thousands and thousands of years of sentience could follow whilst he was, by infinitesimal degrees, buried ever-more deeply. Buried alive. Then he'd move into geological time, still trapped, still aware. If being an irreparably injured immortal means being bound to perfectly preserved remains, he wonders when that attachment would end. When would he finally slip his immortal coil? Would it be when he became fossilised; at one with the rock, or would he remain in that mineralised state for millions of years until an imprint of his broken body became exposed by geological shifts, and then dissipated by erosion. Or perhaps, worse still, his mortal flesh might resist fossilisation in his journey through geological time and he'd reemerge from the rock to be eaten alive by the next dinosaurs. It's bewildering to contemplate the point at which he'd cease to be, but when you've been living a reclusive, lonely existence for hundreds of years, you spend a lot of time thinking about how and when it will end.

I first encountered The Immortal when he was wandering around inside our house at about three in the morning. I was seven years-old. We lived in splendid rural isolation and never locked our exterior doors at night. This suited the curiosity of

The Immortal who liked to keep a close eye on his only neighbours. Our home was the last occupied shell of what had once been his thriving community. I've no idea why ours was the only property selected for reinhabitation. Perhaps it was the biggest. During my family's tenure, it grew bigger still – with my father making changes to the farmhouse he bought pretty much from the moment we moved in. Dad was a serial extender. He'd just finished building an extra room downstairs which we called the Sun Room because it was over-eagerly fitted with huge windows and captured an abundance of sunlight. The interior door that opened into the Sun Room, was placed where the back door of the house had been when we moved in. The Sun Room had no exterior door; there wasn't space for one between all the windows.

I was sleeping in the Sun Room because my Gran was staying with us and she was in my bed. I woke just before three in the morning and felt a bit spooked. I went over to this new internal door, which had been left open on my request while I fell asleep, and pushed it firmly shut. Feeling safer having sealed myself off from the dark downstairs, I got back into bed, pulled the top sheet and blankets up to my chin and snuggled down. A few minutes later the door opened and The Immortal was there. He had one hand on the door handle, and one on the door frame. He was frozen in shock; bewildered by my presence; and saddened by the relentless changes in the house since we'd moved in. His expression clearly telegraphed a thought: that back door had served several generations. It had been fine for many families; why not mine? I went in an instant from drowsy and disorientated to hysterically alert. My behaviour set him even further aback. Some kid, screaming like he'd seen a ghost, was lying on a camp bed in the middle of a glass-obsessed, seemingly functionless room. A mature, bountiful greengage tree had until recently stood exactly where I lay. The immortal had feasted off that greengage tree for more autumn nights than he cared to count. He had planted it himself one night forty or so years earlier, shoving a sprouting greengage stone into an unused patch of overgrown garden. Concealed by the dark, he'd nurtured that tree to bountiful wonderment. It was no more. Rumbled and afraid of being caught, he fled. I raced upstairs and refused to ever sleep in the Sun Room again.

For years after that incident, I was petrified of supernatural beings. At the age of eleven, when school friends were happily watching 18-Rated horrors on VHS and Betamax, I still couldn't watch Dr. Who without periodically retreating behind the sofa or a large cushion. My sister taunted me about that. Then, six years after I had, she saw The Immortal. Within two further years, my gran and a baby-sitter had also caught him carrying-out his late night patrols. They all wrote him off as a ghost. He never looked like a ghost to me. I knew ghosts from my dreams. I'd also been a lot closer to him than anyone else. I saw the complex expression that appeared on his face in response to seeing me. Ghosts don't respond to circumstances they come across. Ghosts are locked into one emotional state – usually morbid, self-obsessed misery. And there was other evidence that led me to conclude that The Immortal was more than pure spirit. He'd opened a door. He ran off, frightened of closer contact with everyday folk. He was afraid of the day. In addition to the evidence gleaned from my encounter, all other reports of his behaviour sounded like he was someone carefully curious of the present, rather than trapped in the past.

Once I'd arrived at the conclusion that he wasn't an apparition, I set out to confront him. Even then it took me eighteen months to find him. Or, to be more accurate, it was not until eighteen months of searching, that he deemed me worthy of meeting him. I always searched at night – it didn't take the deductive powers of Sherlock Holmes to realise that his modus operandi was bumming round in the wee hours. At first, my journeys into the dark outdoors were terrifying. After sundown in the countryside, background noise drops significantly in level. This absence of sound becomes a blank canvas onto which vibrant crunches and crackles are painted. Tiny nocturnal footsteps are amplified a thousand times. In the starlit almost-dark, a young mind hears psychopaths and imagines ghosts when badgers bumble and owls orate. Clarity of vision is lost too. Moonlight transmogrifies hedges and rocks into monsters and demons. Night in the country is no longer the realm of mortal man – our mastery of the planet is undermined by weakened senses. But, once you've got used to the sensory difference of darkness, you become part bat, and your ears become your greatest weapon. You can see round corners and through trees. After a year and a half of wandering around in blurred blacks and heavy imposing greys, my night senses, although a pale imitation of The Immortal's, were tuned-in enough to earn me my second encounter. We met at midnight, both supping chuckling water from a tiny waterfall in an abandoned cider apple orchard. We've stayed in contact ever since.

I'm the only living person in The Immortal's life right now – have been since Stuttering Eric died three years ago. Like The Immortal, Stuttering Eric was prone to wandering the local countryside late at night. He lived three miles down the road in a little village that had escaped the trauma that shrivelled ours. He walked everywhere. He had to walk. He wasn't capable of passing a driving test – he wouldn't have been capable of doing much more than applying and releasing a handbrake. And he had no money to pay for taxis because he didn't work. He wasn't lazy, he just never expected to earn a living – growing-up in an era when 'simple' people were expected to while away their lives sitting on a bench somewhere, watching the more capable world go by. That given role affected him hugely. He had no regard whatsoever for normality. Or time. He was immune to the vagaries of night and day. It always seemed apt to me, therefore, that he was the only regular in the local pub who was as unintelligible at closing time as he was at opening time. Stuttering Eric.

Stumbling around that drinking den was one of the two situations in which you'd find Eric. The other was when he was wandering the countryside – something he did at all times of day and night. His most regular routes were: heading into town, where he collected out-of-date newspapers; off to meet his 'girlfriend' in the ivy-covered house next to the old church by the river (she made him cups of tea); heading home from town; and to and from the pub. He was a mobile local landmark and, like all recognised local landmarks, the extent of most people's interaction with him was staring at him from a distance. Stuttering Eric had five things in his life; his home, free newspapers, The Star, his girlfriend (who was as old and as simple as he was) and his best mate – The Immortal. The Immortal is an incredibly intelligent man. Stuttering Eric, as I've just explained, wasn't. But they got on like a silver spoon-fed aristocrat gets on with his brawling, working class gamekeeper. Their obvious differences were so contradictory that they attracted zero consideration. What mattered was their commonalities. They would sit enjoying one another's company for hours at a time. I would marvel at how they could look at the moon together, without talking, for hours on end. One would grunt in appreciation at its beauty, the other would grunt back in acknowledgement. Intellectually they were a billion miles apart, spiritually they were joined at the hip.

I visited The Immortal last week. It's the first time I've seen him since Stuttering Eric died. Stuttering Eric was killed when a terrapin, caught from a local aquatic centre by a buzzard, was dropped from an immense height. It is speculated that the raptor released it when the reptile nipped one of its claws with it's razor-sharp beak. The terrapin struck Eric on the top of his skull, and a shard of its shell was driven through his cranium into his lethargic, cross-wired brain. They found him three days later in the middle of a pea field. He'd probably been scrumping. The police left that suspicion out of their report for the sake of his relatives.

I presumed Stuttering Eric's death would have badly affected The Immortal. It didn't. Not in the slightest. A long time ago he told me that a death is like a pile of dog shit on a pavement. If you see it for what it is, all you need do is make a slight altera-tion in your short-term journey and, before you know it, you've forgotten all about it. But if you stumble into it, put your foot it in, it'll be with you for ages – a nauseating stench you can't seem to get rid of. And even after you've washed it away, the impression it's made upon your senses will still linger. Although I knew The Immortal was phlegmatic, I'd previously assumed it was just that he'd seen enough of life not to be disturbed by it's highs and lows. It wasn't until we toasted goodbye to that cheery simpleton, and I saw his calm, coldhearted gaze, that I realised The Immortal had an impregnable heart. He told me he felt no emotion at the loss of his long-term companion. It was when he saw my bewilderment that he explained to me the secret of immortality: whilst time is a constant, ageing is not; you age when something upsets you. Each little droplet of distress is moisture extracted from a once-full ripe fruit; the more that evaporates, the more diminished you become. We perceive this process as ageing. When you die of old age, you are a battered, miserable, shrivelled-up prune; the life sucked out of you.

The Immortal lost his entire family, and his close friends and neighbours, to The Plague. He was one of the lucky few who were immune to the disease. By the age of nine, he was the only one left alive in the thriving hamlet that once spanned our land and the wood that surrounds it. When he buried the last corpse – his mother – he promised he'd never let himself feel loss again. Never be a victim. It took him many years of effort to isolate himself from emotional pain, but he achieved it in the end. As I mentioned before, the last time he felt a glimmer of distress, the last time he aged, was when he abandoned the complete upkeep of his family home.

The Immortal's defeat of emotional vulnerability was completed more than two centuries ago. He purged himself of it so completely that he is unable to feel any kind of heartache whatsoever. I asked him if I should attempt to sever myself from human emotion and become immortal too, so that we could be mates forever. He strongly advised against it.

GUINEA PIG KILLER

When I was young, I allegedly killed one or more guinea pigs. I say allegedly because I was somewhere between two-and-a-half and three-and-a-half years old at the time, which is the current ages of my two children. When they're adults, I doubt they'll remember any of the things they do now. Nevertheless, the guilt of the guineapigicide hangs around my psyche like a post-lamb bhuna fart at the back of a non-air conditioned coach on a cold, windows-shut day. And it's not only guilt that haunts me. There's anger there too. I'm angry at many things that relate to the alleged incident. I'm angry that I may have wilfully executed a small number of innocent guinea pigs. I'm angry that something of which I have no memory has been attributed to me – without me being able to offer reason, justification or contrary evidence. And I'm angry that the lives of one or more pet rodents were ended prematurely at some point in my family's history. If one of my children killed a guinea pig, I'd be really angry with them. I'd be upset that they had the capacity to be so cruel, and upset that I'd failed to help them develop a sense of right and wrong. There will always be cruel, nasty fuckers on this earth who take delight in producing child sociopaths. I'm not one of them. For all these reasons, I hugely resent ever being labelled as the family guinea pig slayer.

My family don't go on about it all the time. In fact, it wasn't until I was about to write this story and mentioned it to my mother that, with difficulty, she remembered it at all. My sister easily remembered it though, when I asked her. And I remember it (the label that is, not the event). For all I know, my mother may have pretended to have forgotten about it when I mentioned it recently. Perhaps she knows how much the stigma has scarred me. Damaged me. She hadn't always struggled to recall the story – I clearly remember a time when the accusations of my guinea pig killing were regularly bandied about. Reminding me of my alleged cruelty was the over-used ultimate familial put-down; the fail-safe way to stop me in my tracks and shut me up. I hated being called a guinea pig killer and being unable to defend myself. I remember, back then, trying to see into the past; to visit the moment when the guinea pigs died – just to know the truth. But if I *was* present at the moment of their forced expiration, I never could recollect it. My earliest memories are of trying in vain to picture the incident. Infuriatingly, my desperate attempts to visualise the event, have made me even *less* clear about whether or not I was present at the time of the violent deaths of those cumbersome rodents. Years of soul-searching produced hypothetical reenactments that have left me unsure as to whether I'd actually seen it, or my attempts to do so had created false memories.

If you sense my frustration, believe me, the annoyance you're picking-up is just a pitiful fraction of the bitter angst I bore as a child and retained as a young man. What's helped me overcome the guilt, anger and torment, is the realisation that since the age of three, I've been responsible for the deaths of countless other animals. I eat meat. Scores of pigs, cattle and lambs have had their lives cut short because of my appetite. I've eaten a couple of rabbits, a few wood pigeons, plenty of cute little ducks, hundreds upon hundreds of chickens, and even bits of goose. I've scoffed fish from rivers and the sea. I've smashed limpets from rocks as bait for rock-pooling on holiday. I've boiled alive mussels, crabs and lobsters – I've even swallowed living oysters straight from the shell. I've callously devoured mammals, fish, invertebrates, amphibians (specifically their back legs) and birds. And I don't feel guilty about a single one of those lost lives. I've even killed without the excuse of needing to eat. I've swatted flies, drowned caterpillars for my Nan (picking them off her roses), trapped and poisoned less-cuddly rodents, and bought dried fish as ornaments. In France, a few years back, at about three in the morning on a motorway circumnavigating Paris, I hit a creature with my car whilst travelling at one hundred and thirty kilometres per hour. The animal ran out in front of my vehicle at about one tenth of the distance of the beams of my headlights. I couldn't avoid it. I felt a bump as I ran over it. I don't know what it was. There's a remote possibility it was an intelligent alien life form – or the pet of an intelligent alien life form. In that high-speed frozen instant, it looked like nothing I'd ever seen before. And it moved like a cross between ET and a Gremlin. And yet the ending of that rare creature's existence doesn't trouble me in the slightest. I'd actually forgotten about it until I started listing all the animate life forms I've killed. I don't feel remorse about its death. It was an accident. Other animals have suffered and died for me, too; animals used to test the cosmetics and toiletries I used to use; and animals killed during medical research carried-out on my behalf. But although thinking about all the death I've sown helps, I'm still haunted by the premature termination of those cruelly slaughtered guinea pigs.

For some reason, the execution of creatures I have no memory of, from a time when I was quite forgivably relatively amoral, still upsets me. And it's a complicated set-up. Later investigations of their expiration revealed considerable ambiguity about how the guinea pig, or pigs, died. These facts further fuelled my journey away from the guilt. Apparently the fluffballs were kept outside in a run constructed from short, solid wooden boards that my unqualified carpenter father had slung together. According to those who claim to remember the story (most notably my sister, who taunted me endlessly with this terrible and unproved conviction, along with my mother and father, who obviously had to attend to the squished corpses), the guinea pigs may have simply been crushed by one of the roughly-assembled planks of solid wood falling on them. The other postulations are: that I'd jumped over one of the fences to play with them, accidentally landing on them; and the obvious conjecture that in an act of unprovoked savagery, I'd slaughtered them by stamping on them as they darted around the run, desperately trying to evade me. Of course, neither of these alternative possibilities ever felt viable. If the fence had crushed them, blown over by the wind or collapsing due to poor fabrication, the bodies would have been underneath it. Basic investigation of this evidence would have proclaimed the verdict, and I'd never have been accused of killing them. Furthermore, if they'd been bumped-off by me accidentally landing on them, it's highly unlikely that I'd have killed more than one guinea pig. Whilst I cannot confirm the number of mortalities, it was always implied that a minor massacre had taken place, in which case no unfortunate landing of small black leather shoes could have been responsible. I am therefore left with a Gordian knot that I cannot untie. A knot of historic detail, or lack of it, that becomes more entangled that every time I struggle with it.

The deepest consolation I have found, is the belief that there must be a simple, logical reason why I could never remember any of the detail of this incident: I propose that I have no memory of the guinea pig slaughter because I was never there. This is a suspicion I can remember having from the earliest days. It isn't me grasping for straws; it's that sound lasting philosophy, Occam's Razor – that things tend toward simplicity. The truth is generally the simplest possible explanation. I didn't do it. I didn't do it because I can't remember watching them die.

I think my sister killed the guinea pigs in a fit of psychotic, murderous rage displaced from something she couldn't exact revenge on – probably me. She has always been manipulative. She is eighteen months older than me. That age difference made her mature enough at the time of the murders to be able to construct a false story about my culpability. If she did kill them, that would explain why she was always my greatest accuser. She knew having a scapegoat is the best way to throw the inquisitive off their trail. An apparent solution will encourage amateur sleuths to abandon the effort of investigation. Knowledge of her guilt might also be the reason why, thirty five years later, she is the only member of my family who appears to recollect the affair with ease.

And while I'm on the subject of clearing out skeletons of juvenile criminal behaviour from my family closet; when I was about ten years-old, someone turned off the deep freezer in our shed. Mum used to freeze fruit and vegetables from the farm on an industrial scale. A summer and autumn of stewing and freezing would take us through the following winter and spring. That year it didn't. All the produce was all ruined. My sister was the only one to claim she'd seen something suspicious – namely me entering the shed at around the time the freezer must have been turned off. I endured weeks of punishment for the food that went to waste. I don't remember turning it off. And then, when I was about seven or eight, two packets of marshmallows went missing from a drawer in the kitchen. Unusually, my sister was actually the prime suspect for that offence. She loved marshmallows, but has always denied committing the crime. Mention it to her now, thirty years later, and she'll still fly into a rage. I have always been convinced she stole those marshmallows. In fact, thinking back, I'm sure I saw her eating them in her bedroom.

FAT TOM

I knew a bloke who ate his children. I knew him as a boy and teenager. His name was Tom. He was in my junior class at school. He was fat. Really fat. He looked like a comedy fat kid – straight out of a children's comic. The fat kid in a comic who's always sneaking off and stuffing himself full of pies. And he did just that. I've seen some unsettling things in my time; bits of blown-up human bodies; a UFO; someone suck their own cock; ghosts; a beheading; a woman shitting in another woman's mouth; a man with live maggots in a wound; and a motorcyclist lying 100 metres further down the road than his bike and left leg. But the most disturbing thing I've ever seen was Fat Tom stuffing his face.

We were cutting open pigs' eyes by the oil burner in our classroom. One kid fainted and was allowed to go and sit in the corner. A minute or two later, Tom complained that he was also feeling sick, and asked if he could go to the toilet. Teacher excused him. Ten minutes later, Tom hadn't returned. Concerned, Teacher sent me to the loo to see if he was alright. I returned with the news that he wasn't there. Teacher didn't trust me, so told us all to stay in the class and checked for herself. She returned believing me; and worried. It's very possible that slicing up eyeballs was not actually on the syllabus for nine year-olds and I think she was more worried about getting into trouble with the authorities for encouraging under-age butchery than she was about the possibility that something terrible had happened to Tom. Whatever the reason, she quickly organised search parties and we spread out like little Scooby Doo gangs, determined to find the fat git.

It wasn't a big school, so when one of the search parties excitedly screamed their discovery of him, the rest of the class came flocking. We ran from all corners of the building and its playgrounds like thirty seagulls honing in on a bucket of fish guts tipped from a trawler. The target for our attention was in the cloakroom. A crowd of onlookers had formed at the entrance. Teacher barged over-exuberantly through the melee to get to the heart of the matter. Eager to see what was causing the commotion, I snuck in behind her, moving through the flash-mob like an impudent car following an emergency vehicle through busy traffic. I arrived just after her; a tin can tied to the back of a wedding car making an emergency stop. We were met with a pitiful vision. Fat Tom was sat on the floor below a row of coats hanging by their hoods, weeping whilst stuffing his chubbery face with other children's packed lunches. He sat cross-legged like a distraught chunky Buddha. He was surrounded by lunch paraphernalia – opened air-tight boxes, empty wrappers and ripped-open school bags which were strewn all around him like the nervously slung offerings of devout followers. Like a Buddha, he'd reached a state all of his own; achieved though relentless guzzling rather than meditation. Unlike a Buddha, he would not be immune to the judgement of mortals; and the packages at his feet did not indicate devotion – they indicated trouble. His pouring tears were not blinding enough to obscure his impending retribution, but his clouded vision did prevent him from seeing the intensity of the suffering he was generating. I saw it, I felt the pitiful misery of Tom's existence to the deepest fathom of my soul. The rest of the immature crowd felt it too. We stared, dumbstruck, at the desperateness of his predicament as he bawled out humanity's pain. OK, you could argue that I'm being a little over-the-top, and that the fat fuck was simply crying because he couldn't stop himself gorging stolen lunches; an act that was going to get him into trouble. Believe me, it wasn't that simple, we onlookers could see that his distress ran far more deeply than fear of punishment. If it had been just that, getting rumbled by his entire class body would have stopped him. But being surrounded by multiple eye witnesses (who were also victims) was not enough to make him desist. As far as he was concerned, he had risked the journey to Olympus, found ambrosia, and would damned-well pleasure himself with it until the harpies carried him off. A posse of excited schoolmates was no more than a chorus for his tragic comedy. He sensed we were all following the script, holding back from the main stage, so he continued to stuff his face as we watched in awe at his emotive performance; tears running in stinging streams down his bloated red cheeks.

"Put that food down!" barked Teacher. He didn't. He panicked at the prospect of losing his bounty and became more desperate, grabbing ever more frantically at the consumables littered around him. He continued to sob with self-loathing, while simultaneously compounding his grief by shovelling the stolen grub down. I felt his pain in the bottom of my stomach. It cramped up empathetically at the pitiful sight of the boy and his disorder (years later, right up until the moment I learned he'd eaten his children, hearing Tom's name would always take me straight back to that cloakroom and I'd see him, vividly, tamping food down his throat

- an image which would retrigger my initial emotion and make my abdominal muscles tighten). Frustrated by Tom's public subordination, Teacher resorted to violence. She tried to drag him away from the scene of his crime. But he was in a feeding frenzy, and he was too big and she too petite for her to forcibly extract him. So she dashed off and returned with a big male teacher (an ex first-class rugby player) and the brawny sleeves-always-rolled-up caretaker. They easily sliced their way through the animated crowd to find Fat Tom face down in his seventeenth course – my Mum's cold, homemade shepherd's pie. Without a word they grabbed him and attempted to drag him from the cloakroom. Even for those tough cookies, he was a handful. He had the strength of a madman and the wriggliness of a possessed child. Like an oil-drenched pygmy-hippo-sized escaped toad evading zookeepers, he managed to launch himself at a couple more food items before they successfully got a grip of, and extricated him. Throughout his capture and removal, he screamed like a harpooned walrus. It was a tragic thing to witness. Although we kids had been shouting at him to leave our food alone, no one laughed (as children often do at the misfortune of others). It disturbed us all too much. The shouting was simply an attempt to defend our lunches; "leave that alone!" and "that's my Wagon Wheel!" rather than "fat freak!" or "piggie!".

Within a few weeks of Fat Tom's plundering of his schoolmates' lunches, he disappeared from our school. We were told that he needed special education. He went to some school I'd never heard of before, miles and miles away. It must have been residential; he couldn't have commuted. During my last couple of years in junior school, I'd think of him now and again. That fat lonely bastard, already terribly marginalised, now additionally separated from his mother and two brothers. I'd imagine how terrible it would be to be removed from a situation where you're getting a rough time, only to be slung into a new environment where you'll get a far worse one. When I next saw Fat Tom, on the first day at senior school, I hardly recognised him. From that day on he was just plain Tom. In fact, if he'd attracted another adjective to precede his name, it would have been 'Gaunt'.

Tom had changed. He was a shadow of his former self. He had been one of the 'characters' in junior school – and not just because he was fat. Looking beyond his frame (which you could manage in reasonably wide school corridors), there was a lot to Tom in his younger years. He was funny. That may seem a cliché, but how many more funny fat people have you met than funny skinny people? And he wasn't just a cheap one-line joke merchant; his humour and personality ran as deep as the blubber on his belly. He was a comic original – the kind of kid you never forgot. It didn't take a pillaging trip to the cloakroom to make him memorable; he was a fascinating individual before that impromptu banquet. But I have to concede, much of his amusing nature was probably the product of the tortured mind that resulted from his ravenous appetite. He was continually torn between wanting to eat and not wanting to be fat – pressure he felt compelled to make light of. He was a classic example of a victim who uses originality and humour to combat their handicaps. Although he was fat and fucked-up, he wasn't dangerously disturbed. The conflicts he dealt with turned him into a fun, interesting, distinctive personality – not a psychopath. And even that wasn't the whole story. Tom was made from more than fat and laughter – he had sparkle too. Straight laced and uncomplicated people never have sparkle. Square pegs fit comfortably into square holes and draw no attention to themselves. Tom was round, he didn't fit in. People who don't slot easily into prescribed holes sparkle because they rub against the grain. That's what makes them shimmer when the surrounding crowds are dull. New Tom, Gaunt Tom, had no sparkle. Whatever had happened to him at wherever he'd been, stole that from him. The first day I saw him at senior school, it was instantly apparent that he'd lost three things: his fat tissue, his infective sense of humour and his sparkle. And during the remaining youthful years that I knew him, he regained none of them.

By this point in the tale, you might be feeling sorry for Tom. Well don't forget, when he was forty-seven, he was jailed for life for eating five of his children. Whatever happened to him in those intervening academic years definitely affected him. But lots of children receive special schooling, as well as other sorts of interference from local authorities, and very, very few such children end up eating their own offspring. I don't blame the social care system for making Tom a monster, I blame him. His kids weren't force-fed to him.

Prior to arrest, Tom and his numerically fluctuating family had lived on a small island. It was owned by an incredibly wealthy aristocrat, an Earl. Tom was the gamekeeper. A few times a year this aristocrat would visit the island to bag a few puffins. This is illegal, but his family bore puffins in their hereditary crest. They had been hunting them since the middle ages and the aristocrat believed in keeping the family tradition alive. They could get away with it because they always invited senior members of the local judiciary on the trips, and the Island was hidden from public view. Tom was tasked with maintaining the island's natural environment. He never asked for payment. All he seemed to require was puffery about how well he was doing job. His actual motivation for the job was being left alone to live life his way. 'His way' involved remaining as isolated as possible from mainland life, raising several children and, as was ultimately revealed, consuming some of them. His wife shared the same values – I've no idea what made her as weird as her husband.

They got caught-out because the son of the old Earl had played with one of Tom's children when they both were boys. When the new Earl returned for the first puffin hunting trip since his father's death, he decided to go and find the young man he'd met years before. He was told the boy had died. When he asked about whereabouts of the grave in order that he could pay his respects, he was told there wasn't one. Suspicions were aroused. It transpired that although several children had died, not one proper burial had taken place. They found a few scattered bones, but the majority of the skeletons had been cast into the sea and washed away, or used as jewellery or tools, or burnt in fires. These processes would have erased any evidence of mortal injury that may have existed. The absence of damning forensic evidence made a murder trial impossible. In order to convict someone of murder, you generally need a body. Tom had eaten all of those. And not on his own. His wife, by her own testimony, had shared them with him. And his four surviving children had consumed amounts of their siblings too.

Tom and his wife's legal representatives claimed that all the ingested children had died of natural causes. They claimed that, living at one with nature in a self-sustaining environment as they were, Tom and his wife simply believed that nothing should go to waste. The media coverage lasted for months. In all that time, the headline that captured everyone's imagination was "If the worms can eat them, why can't we?" Some sick individuals printed T-Shirts and badges bearing that quote. Go to the wrong parts of town and you'd see them everywhere. A death metal band even gave an album that title. In case it isn't immediately obvious, Tom used that rhetorical question to argue it was his and his family's right to dine on their own dead. The lead prosecutor had asked Tom why he thought he had this right. Tom responded with a challenge; he questioned why it would have been acceptable to bury his children and let the worms eat them; cast them into the sea and let sea creatures eat them; let fire consume them; or even lay them outdoors to be picked-at by crows and rats – but not use their lifeless corpses to sustain his surviving, struggling family; "If the worms can eat them, why can't we?" – I can see his argument. But although Tom and his wife had removed themselves from mainstream living, they couldn't escape the long arm of the law. Their island is part of our national territory, and that arm reached out across the salty water. He tried to use the foam-topped waves as a smokescreen, claiming in defence that his children had died of natural causes. His wife also said their children had died of natural causes. Their remaining children backed them up. But then they'd been living from hand-to-mouth on that island for up to twenty years, so they were only ever going to stand by one another. Tom and his wife were jailed for life for multiple acts of cannibalism. Their offspring, entirely raised on the island and isolated from mainstream morality, could hardly be penalised for breaking laws they had no knowledge of. But, unsurprisingly, like Tom had been as a child, they were all taken into special needs institutions, where they remained until they reached majority.

I attended much of the trial and I watched as the vilified

family were led away. It purged me of the overpowering discomfort of rewitnessing Tom's desperate gluttony every time I thought of him. That sickening childhood memory has been replaced with the ironic realisation that whilst their father's childhood-obsession with food had led him to seek total escape from social scrutiny, his anarchic adulthood has condemned his living offspring to a future defined by it. And I can't help thinking that none of their misery would ever have manifested if that fat little boy had only been able to resist the forces that tempted him to sin back in junior school – the mouth-watering aromas emanating from Pandora's lunchbox.

THE EXPANDING HOUSE

Frank's fifty-something nephew pulled his near-empty people carrier alongside the pavement outside his uncle's house. Frank mournfully edged himself out. He insisted his nephew sit tight. He'd already refused numerous proposals to be escorted to his widower's dwelling. He wasn't going to fail at the final hurdle. Unaccompanied, he crossed the grey narrow public walkway, then crunched his way, head bowed, up his gravel driveway. He advanced deliberately. Alone. Silent, apart from his measured footsteps and muted grief-laden breath. His nephew pulled away when Frank reached the entrance of his home. Deserted, he handled his door keys with the dexterity of a gloveless Red Army partisan in midwinter. After a minute or two of embarrassing struggle, he managed to unlock the front door. With a shaking hand, equipped with semi-petrified fingers, he pushed it creakingly open.

Frank stepped inside, expecting to be greeted by the instantly recognisable, welcoming parquet-floored hallway he'd trod slipper-shod countless times. He presumed that in stark contrast to his newly single future, the hall of his home would be unchanged; stretching, as ever, it's familiar path to the lounge and kitchen doors at the far end, with a third door halfway down on the right next to the coat stand. But it wasn't. Like his life, the hallway had changed, but while he'd lost something, the passageway had gained. It had grown a new door. There were now two doors on the right hand side of the hallway – one on one side of the coat stand, and a second on the other. Frank thought about turning on the spot (like he had during hinterland drill practice) and charging as fast as he could down the street to announce this black magic. But he checked himself. That would mean deserting his home. And his home (well, the vast majority of it since the arrival of this new door) was the main tangible connection he had to the woman he'd loved dearly since their meeting at a tea dance over half a century earlier. It was a building crammed with shared memories and joint possessions. Every dash of paint, every minor alteration, was infused with their history. It was a monument to them – an evolving, almost living version of the stone memorial in the forest dedicated to his young fallen comrades. If he retreated, his recent loss would be doubled. He didn't run. He'd faced fear-inspiring forces before and not run. He wasn't in a mood to change the habit of a lifetime (actually, for the record, he couldn't run. Arthritis had seen to that. If he had made his escape, it would have been with an agitated fast walk that would have made him look like an old wino being attacked by a swarm of bees). He stayed to face the music, gingerly pushing the door to behind him.

For the first time since his darling love had been hit by a drunk driver, he was home. He had the house to himself. The silence of the almost empty building struck him like the pressure wave of an explosion in sub-zero conditions. Frank was stunned. He stood in the little porch for far longer than he otherwise would have. Not only did he have to take in the magnitude of life as a heart-broken single man, he also had to work out how to respond to his home's bizarre growth. His immediate impulse was to walk up to the door and open it. But, there could be anything behind that door. He wasn't as nimble as he once was. Age had wearied him. He accepted his diminished robustness. And yet it was with his ailing frame that he'd have to confront the greatest challenges of his life so far: his wife's sudden death; the anger he felt towards the lout that smashed her fragile body; and the readjustment he'd have to make to living alone. All in all, he had enough to deal with. The door had materialised shut, not open. There was probably a reason for that. He would leave it closed for the time being.

Frank strode down the corridor, breaking with tradition by leaving his shoes on (he hadn't always taken his shoes off because his wife told him to. He'd done it because he'd always wanted to. Taking your shoes off before you walk into a home was a value they'd both always shared). And with his house sprouting new architectural features, he might have to make a sharp exit. There would be no shame in that – any old soldier knows the difference between a retreat and a tactical withdrawal. Empowered by that thought, he left them on. He kept his woolen trench coat on too, as his heels clutted down the hardwood hallway. He had built up sufficient courage to march past the new doorway, but he sure as hell wasn't going to hang around next to it. The coat stand was right next to the mysterious portal; and he'd have to linger there it if he planned to disrobe. That just wasn't necessary. So he didn't. He marched straight ahead, eyes forwards, like a reserve heading for the front to replace fallen buddies. His forward encampment was the kitchen. On arrival he put the kettle on. He needed the drink that is vastly better at thawing a chilled spirit than anything alcoholic – a cup of tea. Frank spent the remainder of the late afternoon and early evening in the kitchen.

He sat purposefully on his chair, staring at his wife's empty one, supping occasional slurpfuls of warming brew. He tried to eat, but managed only a handful of fig rolls. He ate them straight from the mess-tin shaped biscuit tin.

When the clock in the lounge chimed ten, he headed upstairs for bed. He and his wife had generally stayed up much later than that – retiring at midnight or even half-past. But without his usual domino, bridge, or conversation partner, there seemed little reason to remain alert. He certainly wasn't going to go to bed late just for the sake of it. As he passed the new door, it frightened him for the first time. He was unsettled when he'd first seen it. Confused. Perplexed. But it wasn't until that rectangular egress was bathed in darkness, that it really scared him. Transformed by gloom, it took on the shape of the doorway to a torture chamber he remembered from long ago. Spooked, he decided to move quickly past it. As he did so, his leather-soled foot skidded on the polished floor blocks. For a moment he imagined himself slipping and violently crashing down on the floor, poleaxed, then some giant ghoulish trapdoor spider flinging the new door open and springing onto his pitiful, immobilised self. This didn't happen. The slip wasn't that bad. He easily regained his stride and strode past it, vowing to always take his shoes off in future. There was a good reason for wearing rubber-soled slippers around the house.

He had plenty to think about as he lay in bed that night. The door threw up all sorts of quandaries, which kept him awake. He heard the clock chime half-past ten, eleven, half-past eleven, twelve and half' midnight before eventually dropping off to sleep. It was not his first night of troubled insomnia. Even before the new door had appeared, he'd been robbed of the restful head-space with which to focus on the loss of his soul-mate. During the first few days convalescing at his nephew's, and throughout the wake, and during the funeral proceedings, he'd been preoccupied by thoughts of the drunken yob who'd ploughed into his wife. Mown her down on a pelican crossing. A clearly marked, fully functional, flashing beacon-flanked crossing for god's sake. That scumbag had a list of petty offences to his name – including two previous convictions for drunk driving, both of which had resulted in driving bans. The soon-to-be-murderer had leapt into his car fleeing the wrath of the Carpenter's Arms' landlord (Frank didn't blame the landlord; he'd just had a barstool thrown at him). There was cruel, cruel irony in the name of her work-shy killer's choice of drinking den. That murderous drunk-driver had never worked a decent days work in his life. Frank had. He'd hardly ever stopped. Straight after putting his life on the line to protect the innocent, he took an apprenticeship and worked till he was sixty seven (he'd been fit enough to work for longer, but his wife had implored him to retire). Throughout his post-war career, Frank had worked as a carpenter. If anyone deserved to be relaxing in the Carpenter's Arms, it was him – not the idle bastard who slaughtered his dearest. Frank hated his wife's killer like he'd never hated anyone in his life before – including during the wartime years of enemy occupation. But the bastard was so despicable, he even managed to deny Frank the simple clarity of thought that hatred should offer. The stupid, sickening irony of the pub's name distracted Frank's anger. It diluted his venom. It robbed him of the power to forge an idol of pure loathing.

When he woke the next morning, confused thoughts racing through his head, one thing gave Frank hope: the possibility that the new door was no longer there. That it had been either an hallucination, or some kind of temporary supernatural anomaly, designed to shock him back into shape. If it had gone; if it had been reabsorbed back into the wall of the passageway, then he could start getting back to normal. He could return to dwelling on the sick coincidence of his wife's killer's local; or even begin to get over it and start creating a new life for himself. He clung to the hope it was no longer there whilst he carried out his morning ablutions; then changed into a casual shirt and v-neck jersey, ready to take on the day. He headed down the stairs, half hoping, half expecting to discover that the ground floor hallway had returned to its normal self. It had not. The new door was still there. Halfway down the stairs, he paused opposite it for the first time, holding onto the banister. The sloping wooden pole served as a safety rail. He gripped it tightly as he cast his eyes downwards.

The door was a perfect match with the original one on the other side of the coat stand. Same height, same wood-panelled construction, and similarly over-thickly coated with several layers of white gloss. But the shiny off-white skin of neither door was perfect. The multiple-layered paint was, in places, chipped down to the dark-stained pine of its stiff body. The doorknobs matched too. Traditional white porcelain doorknobs, each adorned with an overly-vibrant posy of ever-fresh flowers. Initially it surprised Frank to see such a close match. Then he reminded himself that if a house could grow a new doorway, the fact that it could match it to an existing one was a minor detail. He left his viewing gallery and continued to the bottom of the stairs. Before wheeling kitchenwards, he continued to the small porch where he placed his shoes on the shoe rack, then pulled cold slippers onto his grey-socked feet. Frank had had less than twenty-four hours to get used to that new door. And yet, even on the morning of the second day, he found that it disturbed him less. He realised it couldn't be wished away, and there was no avoiding it. If he was going to have to live with it, he might as well try and get used to it. He walked past it and into the kitchen to make himself a slice of toast.

Each extra day made Frank more comfortable with the door. Within a month he found himself walking past it without giving it much of a second thought. It became part of the wallpaper. He never felt the urge to open it, though. The other thing Frank wouldn't do, is invite people to his house. Friends and relatives kept asking if they could pop round, to see how he was, to say hello. He turned them all down. He'd say he wasn't ready to have visitors. He was ready to have visitors. He missed human company. What he couldn't allow to happen, was for anyone else to see the new door. Shocked witnesses would lead to only one thing – him losing the house. So he distributed aural 'do not disturb' signs down telephone wires. The 'trespassers will be rejected' policy worked. He padded the property alone. But the absence of the noise of others slowly began to deafen him. Calls to visit increasingly upset him. He wanted to have guests, but he couldn't. The house that he was desperately trying to come to terms with; to love in its new guise, was becoming his prison. And he was in solitary confinement. So when his oldest niece next called (the one with the three-storey town house he'd always felt at home in), he dropped a hint that although he wasn't quite ready to entertain her and her husband, he'd love to visit them. She took the bait and a week later arrived to collect him in her red sports car. Her car wasn't easy for him to get into, and even harder to get out of, but she knew he loved it. It reminded him of the sports car he and his wife had explored the Highlands in back in the seventies.

Frank was standing guard in front of his three-foot metal gates when his niece arrived. He'd been waiting there some time. When asked, he claimed he'd only just left the house.

He enjoyed a wonderful weekend with the charming couple; it was the first time since his wife's death that he'd felt at ease without her. When it came to an end, he'd been in no hurry to leave, so by the time his niece dropped him off back at his house, it was fairly late. She offered to pop in. He refused; telling her (after she'd helped him to extricate himself from the vehicle) that she should get home as it was late enough already. Seeing his resolve, she didn't pressure him. She got back in the driver's seat, and pulled away with a flamboyant 'see ya' wheel spin. Frank smiled his way up the driveway. His grin lasted, via a shoe/slipper exchange in the porch, all the way to the first floor of his home; but was instantly erased when he reached top of the stairs. There was another new door. This one was between the bathroom and what had been he and his wife's bedroom. The bathroom door was white. As was the bedroom's. This most recent addition was natural wood. It was the stripped-down 'original pine' favoured by affluent couples interested in 'period features'. This second new door literally took his breath away. It was the second strike of a combination punch. The shock of the initial encounter with the first door - a stinging left jab - returned, knocking him off balance. The second door's impact came hard on its tail – a hefty body shot between hip and ribs. He was practically floored. He felt like he'd been whacked in the midriff with a hand-held battering ram then slung into a vacuum. He thought he'd never fill his lungs again. He stumbled backwards, until he was backed up against the handrail at the top of the stairs like a boxer on the ropes. Then, after what seemed like a lifetime of shocked debilitation, he breathed. Painfully.

As he sucked in that first recovery breath, it struck him that the house was angry with him. He had left it on its own again and it had responded in the only way it could to show its displeasure and hurt. It had grown another door. Twice he'd abandoned their love nest. Twice he'd found solace and comfort in another abode. The first time he'd slept at his nephew's; the second time he'd run off with his niece. His home seemed as capable as any woman of responding negatively to being scorned. It was demonstrating its fury. His residence was acting like an unruly puppy that rips up your furniture when you leave it alone for a few hours – it was angry at being temporarily abandoned. It was a self-harming lover, believing its absent partner was having an affair. The doors were his punishment. They were the embarrassing scars. And they were cruel. Whilst they seemed to offer possible new horizons, they did exactly the opposite, because both house and occupant knew they would never be opened. All they would do was keep others away. So although they were unlocked doors, they restricted Frank's world. The irony of their wicked containment was even crueller than that of his wife's killer's boozing venue. He dropped, repentant, to his knees and shuffled over to the door. He gently stroked it like a father strokes a child grieving for its mother. He was a septuagenarian parent rubbing his toddler's nettle-stung skin. He whispered his apologies; his condolences. His home missed its mistress as much as he did. He had behaved appallingly leaving it alone – particularly so soon after her departure. Tenderly, over and over, Frank swore he'd never leave the injured property on its own again. They would live out his final days together in uninterrupted unison.

GEORGINA'S STORIES

Georgina writes stories about writers. That's lame. Writers are supposed to give readers alternative viewpoints on their reality; their lives. That's their job; their duty. And being a writer is an incredible privilege that should not be taken lightly. It's a not only a huge cop-out to write about writers, it's an insult to people who actually graft in the real world. Writing about writers is the mark of a writer who's either too scared or too lazy to take on the real world – either way it's inexcusable.

The only way to comment on the everyday world is to see it from the outside. Seeing life through a writer's eyes gives you the opportunity of considering a different perspective on a world that makes sense to you. That experience enriches your life, illuminating and ultimately reinvigorating your mechanical existence. But in order to benefit from their viewpoint, their subject matter needs to revolve around your mundanity. There's no benefit whatsoever in a writer making fictional writers the focus of their stories. That can't mean anything to anyone. I mean, who's ever actually met a professional writer? Regular people are far too busy struggling with their lives to ever meet writers. If you've ever been to school with a writer or lived near one; way before achieving success they'll have escaped where they came from and abandoned all their true friends. They do that very intentionally in order to gain the perspective they need to do their job properly. And since nobody normal actually knows a writer, why would you want to read a story about one? It's ridiculous. It's like film-makers making films about filmmaking, fishermen catching fish for fishermen or journalists working on trade magazines for journalists.

But what's even more annoying than Georgina writing about writers, is the fact that her best-selling book features a writer who writes about a miserable writer! That's so incredibly self-indulgent it makes my temples throb just to think of it. This so called 'work' is twice removed from real life. It doubly fails to offer any illumination on the real world. It's a disgrace that the damned thing was ever written let alone published. The only valid aspect of that sorry excuse of a book is the fact that the writer that Georgina's fictional writer writes about is depressed. I'm not bloody surprised! He's a construct so fragile that his flimsy existence must be absolute torture. That twice-distanced-from-reality-writer is not even the product of an actual writer's imagination; he's the creation of the creation of someone who ignores the basic duty of their craft. Now you tell me: what could that stupid story possibly mean to anyone?

That said, what annoys me most of all about this story, what *really* gets my goat, is the commercial success it's enjoyed. Georgina has earned a fortune from that book. It's paid for her house; put her children through private school; it takes her and her family on wonderful holidays twice a year; and its a free-entry ticket to any celebrity party she turns up at. I know all this because I read all about Georgina in the gossip magazines. I don't know Georgina personally. I don't know any writers. I'm normal. I'm a struggling unpublished writer. I write three nights a week after I get home from a long hard day's work. And so far the sum total of all my effort is Jack Shit in fiscal terms. And yet Georgina, a so-called writer who hasn't even got the courage or ability to directly comment on our existence, is living a life of splendour and luxury. It beggars belief. I mean, what kind of world are we living in?

GODWATCHING

In the course of human history, three thousand eight hundred and seventy-six people claim to have seen God. Of those, three thousand eight hundred and seventy-five became instantly devoted to their apparition. Carol is the one exception. She saw God but it didn't turn her into a devout follower. And I have good reason to rate the credibility of her claim above that of all the others. Without the detail of this tale, you might find that perplexing. A mere glimpse of something that God *might* have been involved in will change the average hardened disbeliever into an ardent disciple. Believing you've actually seen him has a far greater effect, and usually turns even the most ungodly beings into willing martyrs. And yet Carol didn't just sneak a glance at the him, she stared at him for ages. But she didn't respond by devoting her entire life to singing his praises. In fact, seeing the Big Man had a negative effect on her faith. Post divine vision, her desire to worship actually dissipated. I'm not going to leave you pondering until the end of this tale why Carol responded the way she did. I'll lay it out clear and simple for you right now. She saw God curling out a turd. And she saw it from the end you'd rather not witness that kind of event from. The business end.

Carol was having an out of body experience at the time. She had been having them for as long as she could remember. Carol is what readers of the Fortean Times or tattered car boot sale books on the paranormal would call, an 'Astral Traveller'. Astral travelling is a phenomena in which a person's spirit is able to escape their physical body and roam around the three-dimensional plane. It's a bit like having a remote control ghost, with your eyes sitting in its ghoulish sockets. Not all paranormals are created equal. Like athletes, some possessors of extraordinary powers have greater ability than others. Carol is the Michael Johnson of astral travellers. As a young girl, she projected her astral self around her home; visiting rooms where adults did what adults do when children have been sent to bed. Her gift allowed her to achieve what all kids dream of – escaping the early-night confines of their bedrooms. Whilst her body was incarcerated, her spirit was free. She stopped spiritually wandering round her own home after catching her parents fucking each other violently in the garage. She witnessed them use old rusty gardening tools to cut one another, and suck blood and puss from previously inflicted, infected wounds (incidentally, but unsurprisingly, this incident had a negative and lasting effect on Carol's ability to form adult relationships). After seeing her immediate family way too 'up close and personal', Carol dedicated her teens to exploring more distant human habitations. But people are doing weird and disturbing things behind closed doors all over the world. Several unrestricted years spent observing strangers in their personal spaces, led to her seeing many things she'd rather not have seen, as well as furnishing various police forces with some remarkably well-informed and much appreciated anonymous phone calls. Eventually she realised the sickening exposures to adult interaction were taking their toll on her – making her grow up too fast. So she switched her attention to the natural world, where behavioural acceptability is not an issue.

Unpeopled places satisfied Carol's curiosity into her late thirties. She viewed the depths of the oceans by the bioluminescence of deep-sea marine life; visited the leafy hearts of deep-breathing jungles; sat on the lips of erupting volcanoes and watched receding glaciers calve icebergs into near-frozen seas. Carol's favourite area of study was vertebrates. She easily gained a PhD in animal behaviour and made a good living from lecturing and writing books on the subject. But the ease of her success troubled her for two reasons. Firstly, it's always difficult to feel a sustained sense of achievement from something that comes too easily. And, secondly, she was constantly concerned that someone would rumble her; work out that she knew too much about wildlife with insufficient field research experience. Fortunately, by the time her worries became too much to bear, she was able to retire comfortably on the wealth she'd amassed. Carol abandoned her studies of the planet at work and moved into a remote cottage overlooking a hard-to-reach sandy cove. The perfect place for a recluse.

Carol tried to give-up astral travelling altogether, but it was like a lifelong gardener moving to a tenement block trying to make do without so much as a window box. She was unable to abandon her gift. So she headed for the only place where she couldn't be challenged on how she had obtained her knowledge, because there *was* no knowledge; a place where she wouldn't chance upon people's dark secrets, because there *were* no people. She sent her spirit into outer space.

Before I get to her encounter with God, there are a couple more things you need to know about astral travelling. I didn't tell you about these at the start, because I didn't want to overload you with paranormal technicalities. An astral traveller's range is defined by the magnitude of their gift. Some can only make it

133

down the street; others about as far as Mars or Jupiter. Carol's ability is so immense that there are no limits to how far she can go. You also need to know that, once astral travellers have been somewhere, they can return to that very spot as quickly and easily as you reach to scratch an itch. Their spirits are like homing pigeons with built-in teleporting technology. But, like all other paranormal explorers, Carol was constrained by one limitation – the physical law that restricts us all – time. So, while she visited the outer reaches of space, she could see at each encounter with her bathroom mirror that she was growing older. Alone. Nevertheless, the excitement of breaching new frontiers outweighed Carol's concern that 'real life' was passing her by. On her remarkable journeys she found plenty of new extra-terrestrial things to witness: astounding geological wonders; primitive life; advanced alien species; evidence of lost interstellar empires; even, on a lifeless planet in the Andromeda Galaxy, the remains of several planes and boats that have gone missing in the Bermuda Triangle.

The one thing Carol didn't come across in decades of lonely of inter-stellar astral travel, was an edge. That frustrated her – although, in actual fact, finding an edge to the Universe isn't as easy as you might think. The Universe isn't a simple three dimensional object with obvious sides. You can't just go off astral plane-sailing in one direction until you reach an edge, any more than you can sail to the edge of the earth and drop off it. The Universe is a many bubbled, twisty-turny back on itself thing. It has a billion-trillion-et cetera number of false edges that loop back to other bits. Basically, even if you set yourself the mission of finding an edge, and you posses the ability to hold a map of all of creation in your head, and you can jump to any spot of it in an instant, it's still practically impossible to find an – or the – edge. But, devoid of the distractions of others, and with nothing else to occupy her time, Carol was able to devote herself to this goal. Finally, after many years of obsessed unhealthy reclusivity, her tenacity enabled her to find an – or the – edge. And there, munching away at the extremity of the universe like a pig sticking its head under a barbed-wire fence to reach crops from a neighbouring field, was God.

'Like a pig' is the perfect simile. It's not an attempt to offend followers of various gods – or doting atheist pig-farmers for that matter. It is an accurate description. God was gulping back the non-universe like a voracious hog troughing its last meal. Although edges to the universe are incredibly hard to find, it's not because they're little. They are the very opposite. Although we know it isn't, the universe is so immense that it appears to be infinite. Beyond it is the non-universe, which it touches at every point along its edge, and there's no way of telling how deep the non-universe is. It doesn't take the brains of an Archbishop, therefore, to work out that there is plenty of non-universe out there. Yet with wilful disregard for this obvious logic, God, a celestial entity ranking several levels higher than the aforementioned ecclesiastical underling, was swallowing back gobfuls of the stuff like it was his last meal and it was about to be snatched away from him. In fact, he was eating at such a rate that even his mighty stomach couldn't cope and periodically he turned his immense head to spew. The lumpy bits in God's vomit aren't carrots. Whatever is in his stomach somehow turns the non-stuff beyond the edge of the universe into stuff. Like a drunk student creates pavement pizzas after visiting a kebab shop on the way back to their digs after a night's clubbing, God was bringing up stars and planets which were then forming into spinning circular solar systems. That is how planetary matter is formed. The universe has to be created somehow.

Carol could deal with seeing God puking. Although she'd tired of observing the physical universe after decades of solitary study, she'd always felt it was far better that it existed than didn't. And she'd seen enough weirdness to accept that a gigantic, rotund, bulimic super-being was responsible for its genesis. What turned Carol off a future of dedicated worship was watching God take a crap. After many nightly trips back to the edge of the universe to marvel at its creation, she eventually witnessed him squeezing out a poo. And *my* it took some squeezing – there obviously isn't enough fibre in the non-matter at the edge of the universe to aid regular movement. And, as a result of the immense gravitational forces within his bowels caused by the proximity of enormous amounts of generated matter, God's stools are pretty solid. He gets bunged-up. At first, as he began his defecatory routine, Carol wasn't quite sure what was going on. She saw the supreme being stop eating for the first time in all the months she'd been observing him. His massive blobby body started shaking and shuddering like an outrageously oversized jelly rabbit on a giant washing machine. Then he started tensing up like, well, like someone who's got a bomb in their undercarriage that's way bigger than the bomb hatch. After a few minutes of distress, his crusty sphincter opened wider than a hundred suns. From her position, Carol couldn't help but look up his back passage. She literally saw what he'd had for dinner – aeons ago. Then he squeezed one out. The matter that emerged was so dense that as it piled out of his back end, due to Newton's third law of motion, it pushed God's head and shoulders deep into the non-universe. Seemingly adversely affected by his half-immersion into unreality, and in a state of temporary panic exacerbated by the pressing need to release the gigantic torpedo, God's colossal bumhole anxiously clinched back together, and a super-massive and unfathomably dense piece of matter was severed by his mighty clamping chocolate starfish. Carol saw the payload falling through space for a split second before it ripped straight through the fabric of space-time. The rupture quickly repaired itself, leaving a no more than a tiny-weeny scar – a black hole.

Seeing god poo gave Carol a fresh perspective on life. If the Father of All Creation doesn't have sufficient self-control to resist constant gluttony (one of the seven deadly sins apparently!), then perhaps her parents weren't so warped after all. They were just minor-league transgressors in a universe born of the untreated disorder of the 'Architect of all Matter'. That realisation made her reconsider her childhood pledge to evade intimate human contact – to resist forming relationships.

Carol's happier now than she's ever been. She's given up astral travelling, having seen as much as she wants to of the marvels of the universe. Like a retired Lawrence of Arabia, she's abandoned the vast deserts of open space and turned to rustic simplicity for comfort. Her journey for absolute knowledge was littered with voyeuristic trauma – and the monstrous moon of god, with its cataclysmic cargo, was the straw that broke her paranormal camel's back. She now spends most of her time in her garden, and even welcomes the occasional visitor.

VOICE BOX

Steve stopped speaking. He'd never liked his voice. He decided that actually hated it whilst on a walking holiday in the Dolomites. Twice a year me, Steve and our hotchpotch gang of usual suspects would assemble to spend quality time together. The Italian Alps was our most ambitious destination to date. We'd chosen it after several of us had seen a documentary about it's unique beauty. Barring a couple of notable exceptions, we were all there, wearing stout walking shoes stuffed with thick-socked aching feet.

We'd been hiking for a few days, staying in high-altitude mountain huts, when we arrived at one of the specifically chosen points on our route. It was a rocky platform roughly the size and shape of a baseball diamond and infield, renowned for the echoes you can generate there. The desire to experience its famous effect had been an important factor when choosing our itinerary. We stopped, as parties of hikers have done for centuries, and took turns at shouting something into the ether. The spot lived up to its billing. Our cries were slapped back at us; a multiplicity of split-personality choristers with an incompetent choirmaster. Steve went last. He never pushed to the front of a queue. He was always happy to let the more impetuous members of the group take the lead. Many admired his selfless nature. Others presumed him shy. Whatever his motivation;

going last has its advantages – it means you are presented with the opportunity of being a bit different to everyone else. And this enabled Steve to be a bit more interesting – an issue he was always secretly concerned about. Most of us had shouted something dull and predictable, like "echo" or "hello". Steve shouted "twat" and it set us all giggling. He expected to hear a silly (and not *too* offensive) word bounce off several expansive faces of vertical rock and return in a comical chorus. What he heard was a cacophony of twatty voices accusing him of being a twat. His grating voice was being multiplied and broadcast uncontrollably across many cubic kilometres of fresh mountain air. Enormous monoliths of rock that had stood steadfastly for millions of years were announcing his pathetic, unpleasant, warbly voice to anyone within earshot. We all knew what to expect, but when the first returning soundwave reached Steve's eardrums, he welcomed it as willingly as a lonely Irish farmer hears the wailing of a banshee. He cried. Not openly, but corner-of-the-eye, forcibly-restrained, slowly-welling-tears – silent ones. Much worse misery than the openly pitiable sobbing that attracts instant sympathy and support. Our gang, other walkers, the mountains, the local flora and fauna, all things in range of the inescapable reflected sound waves he set boinging about, were the last witnesses of Steve's nasty, weedy, high-pitched voice. He didn't talk for the rest of the day's trekking. He didn't converse that night at the next hikers' hut. He was silent over breakfast in the morning. He didn't speak to anyone for the remainder of the holiday. He didn't talk on the journey home. The rest of us went through many emotions before getting back. There was bewilderment, confusion, frustration, anger, disappointment, sympathy and acceptance. Whatever our individual perspectives on his behaviour, we would all agree that we went on holiday with a warbly Steve and returned with a silent Steve.

Aside from the fact that he had made a highly unusual conscious decision to stop speaking, Steve had always been a bit odd. He is what you'd categorise as a nerd. Nerds may be generally vilified, but in reality they're like beauty spots; you don't mind having one or two in your life because their distinctiveness adds character and charm. Like interesting points on mountain walks, or seductive birthmarks, their uniqueness appeals. And, let's face it, we are living in the Age of the Nerd. For centuries men with nerdish tendencies would have loitered in the shadows of military heroes, aggressive industrialists and political rhetoricians. These days, nerds are kings. They design the computers that are as important to our lives as water, and look after our fiscal well-being and retirement. We trust nerds with everything, from the technology that keeps planes in the air to the development of medicines that save our lives. Nerds are often very clever. Their gift for, and dedication to a specific area of study, is what prevents them developing a rounded personality. Steve was just such a nerd. He was an electronics genius. He had a very well paid job with a leading computer company, which enabled him to afford a grand, impressive home. When he returned from the Italian trip, he gave up his job and retreated into his house like a hedgehog in winter. But though unemployed, he was far from idle; he gave himself a new purpose – to create an electronic voice box that would generate for him the perfect voice.

It's said that you should never disturb a hibernating animal. It can cause their death. All but one of his old friends treated Steve in the same manner. They'd claim he wanted to be left alone. What they meant was that they couldn't deal with his refusal to speak, his insistence on communicating by handing out a constant stream of roughly scribbled Post-it notes, and his obsessive mission to create an artificial voice. His behaviour disturbed them, undermined their sense of normality. Like anti-Samaritans, they abandoned him. I didn't. I did visit Steve. I was the one friend who didn't give up on him. And, for the record, my visits didn't kill him. While others professed he was better off being left alone, I knew he wasn't enjoying his self-imposed exile. And I can prove it because I've still got a stash of the Post-its he slapped into my hands during visits. Although he was never the life and soul of a party, he'd always revelled in the company of others – particularly our gang, who'd been knocking-around together for years. And he was a crucial part of the crowd, even if it was for slightly dubious reasons. His impressive home was the most regular venue for our parties, and his well-paid job footed the bill for most of the refreshments. Though he knew that not everyone in the circle would want to spend too long trapped in a corner with him, he was a fundamental part of the scene. As a science geek back in school, spending his lunchtimes working alone in the electronics lab, he could never have imagined he'd one day be part of a lively group like ours. Post-echo Steve reverted to type; returning to the lifestyle he'd *not* enjoyed as a teenager. And it wasn't doing him any good.

Each time I visited Silent Steve I'd notice his health had deteriorated further. Although he'd always been light in frame, back in the Dolomites his positive spirit had kept his famously ostrich-like legs moving as fast as the rest of us. But as that spirit fast evaporated, like discarded medical alcohol on a warm chemistry desk, those ostrich legs started to look more like a heron's. Within three months of his withdrawal from society, isolation and reduced sleep had taken their toll on him. Caffeine-pill insomnia and poor nutrition had dried up his skin, sunken his cheeks, turned his eyes bloodshot and underslung them with bags like bloated flesh-coloured crescent moons lying abandoned on their backs. Three months more drudgery left him looking like the star attraction at a Victorian asylum – and his home suitably reflected this new persona. After half a year of committed effort, the work that he'd begun in his garage had spread to every room of his live-in workshop. By then, his endeavour was taking many forms. At the same time as building the device that would provide the perfect voice, he was researching what the perfect voice was. He had countless devices littered about his bachelor's den, recording and playing back the verbal performances from all types of orators; news-readers, union leaders, actors, television presenters, comics, sports commentators, politicians, voice-over artists, business spokes-people, even serial killers interviewed for documentary pro-grammes. Entering his chattering residence was like slipping into the mind of a paranoid schizophrenic – you were relentlessly bombarded by the mixed-up utterances of innumerable earnest voices. He imprisoned himself within a maze of spoken words and, throughout his studies, his only sustenance was instant noo-dles soaked in boiling water.

The last time I saw Steve alive, he looked dead. Actually, I'm a coroner's assistant, and I've seen dead people looking far less dead than he did. He looked like a corpse that had been left to winter in an arctic wilderness; shrivelling in on itself like the freeze-dried fruit in expensive cereals. I tried to get him to see a doctor but he refused, insisting he was well and saying, or rather writing, that his health always deteriorated during an inventive phase. He would also insist that he'd be returning very soon to normal life and well-being, claiming he'd almost achieved his task of creating an 'electronic perfect voice box'. He never did. A month after my last visit, his neighbours complained that a wicked stench from his garage had ruined their five year-old daughter's outdoor birthday party. The police broke in and discovered his wizened corpse lying behind some dusty free-standing paint shelves. They speculated he'd collapsed there after chasing a rat that had been ransacking his Pot Noodle supplies. It took them over an hour of searching the odour-infused house to find Steve's rotting body – having initially chosen not to investigate behind the paint shelves in the garage because they presumed no living being could squeeze behind them.

I was one of the pall-bearers at his funeral, and if it wasn't for the quality of the oak, carrying his boxed-up corpse would have been a one-man job. Most of the old crew showed-up for the funeral – out of guilt I suppose. No one seemed that upset at the ceremony. Steve had no immediate family, being an only child whose parents had long since died. There was, in fact, much more emotion at the reading of his will, which he hadn't changed since his long-time girlfriend Claire left him – about a month before our trip to Northern Italy – for Lloyd; another one of our crowd. As is often the case during times of emotional distress, he never got round to amending his testament. Consequently his ex got the lot. Claire and Lloyd both erupted with unrestrained joy at the executor's announcement. The two of them moved into Steve's place, and living rent-free has enabled Lloyd to achieve the dream he'd always waxed lyrical about – he's built himself a sound booth in the house, which means he rarely has to commute into the city for his voice over work. He sits in what was once Steve's

Dungeons & Dragons room and sends cheesy straplines for over-paid advertising copywriters down ISDN lines.

Claire and Lloyd host the big parties these days, but I don't go to them. I can't bear Lloyd's doorstep greeting; a fake, deep, resonant "Welcome forlorn stranger to our humble abode". It's not half as welcoming as Steve's warbly, high-pitched, but sincere "Hiya, party's buzzing".

SLOW PAINTER

Chris is a slow painter. He's not an artist. Nothing like that. He refers to himself as a painter and decorator. In my mind, painter and decorator is an over-claim. Decorating implies to me some sort of artistic contribution. Chris just paints. He'll advise on types of paint. He'll tell you whether you need gloss or eggshell or matt emulsion. But he doesn't advise on colours. He won't even tell you that two colours don't go together. He doesn't feel that's his remit. He simply paints things the colours you choose. Chris has been painting for a living since he left school. He's painted buildings, inside and out, fences, road markings, park equipment, lampposts. He's never progressed to specialist work like boats or cars. It's not because they're any more difficult, it's because they move and would most likely do so before he'd finish. He's not the most dynamic individual. He's so unmotivated, in fact, that on top of settling for a lifetime of manual labour, he's purposefully selected an unskilled profession. Painting's not like being a bricklayer, or a stonemason, or a plasterer. Anyone can paint. And everyone else who does it for a living is way quicker than he is.

Chris doesn't get a many jobs – he's too slow. But then again, he doesn't need a lot of jobs. What might take an average painter and decorator two weeks will take him a few months. There isn't an exact ratio that you can apply to predict how much slower he'll be than the average painter. That's anyone's guess. But I can guarantee you one thing: he's always taken far, far longer to finish a job than most employers expect him to. And they are usually well aware of his reputation to begin with. You might think no one would ever employ him. But he's stumbled, through luck, into some sort of speciality market. Useless as he is, he has a USP (or unique selling point, if you're not acquainted with marketing terminology).

In his early professional life, many customers got angry and upset at his miserable level of efficiency. Soon his reputation preceded him; warning off potentially frustrated customers. Ironically, his reputation is the only thing about him that ever operated with any level of efficiency and industriousness. Eventually, Chris organically and accidentally spawned a unique customer base. The people who employ him these days, aren't terribly fussed about how long he will take to complete the job they give him. And, hard as it might be to imagine such people exist in the modern hard-working world, they seem to be in sufficient numbers to keep him ungainfully employed. I am told that Chris has an advantage: a warm, enigmatic personality. Some say he's "great to have around". And, if you ask him to paint your house, he's certain to be "around" for a quite a while.

Chris could talk the hind legs off a donkey. Although he achieves very little with his own existence, he's interested in everything about anyone else's. And whilst he operates at the pace of a snail on Valium, I don't get the impression, from what people have told me, that his dithering is a cynical ploy. He seems to genuinely love chatting about pretty much anything you might want to talk about. He's fascinated by the lives of others – their thoughts, things they've got up to, perspectives, tastes. He'll happily talk about any subject of local, national or international news; past or present. And he's as keen to discuss politics as he is business or sport. In fact, there's no area of human activity he won't spend hours gassing over... whilst avoiding, at all possible cost, the danger of actually engaging in any strenuous activity himself. I find it impossible to figure out whether he's slow because he talks so much, or it's *because* he's so slow that he has to talk incessantly to justify the pace at which he works. He charges by the job, so he gains no financial advantage in going slowly.

People must get him in to paint because they fancy having someone around for a while who will listen and talk. Lonely people. If his customers are so miserable that they're happy to wait ages for a simple job to be finished while a stranger encamps in their home, drinking their tea and eating their digestives; that's their business. What perplexes me is how he manages to survive financially on the relatively few jobs he completes each year. He seems to enjoy all the benefits that harder working painter-and-decorators enjoy – a drink down the pub, watching the local football team, decent clothes. He doesn't appear to struggle. I saw his shopping basket once when he was in front of me at the supermarket. He had nice stuff in there. That bothered me. How can someone who works so slowly; someone who obviously hasn't got the first clue about commercial effectiveness, afford to buy fancy foods? He should be living off own-brand 'no frills' stuff. If you're going to make your living painting, surely you'd want to be as quick as you can. The faster you work, the more money you'll earn. And experience ought to enable you to work faster still. Chris has plenty of experience. Yet he's no more qualified now than when he left school forty-odd years ago. And I'd wager that he's still as slow, if not slower, than when he first started. His personal target – ambition, if you can use such a word in relation to him – must be to become the slowest painter in the history of man. Rather than attempt, like a normal person, to improve his performance, he must dedicate himself to painting as little per annum as is humanly possible while still maintaining a career as a painter. He's intentionally regressive. That attitude is shameful as far as I'm concerned – even if his customers do like to chat, and somehow seem to gain from his tiresome company.

If Chris was working for me, his lethargy would send me through the roof. Observing his creeping performance first-hand would get right under my skin. I'm a highly paid pen-pusher, but I could finish a paint job more quickly than he could – whilst only working evenings and weekends. And if his sluggish performance wasn't annoying enough, his incessant drivel would finish me. I get frustrated even catching sight of him lackadaisically dabbing paint onto a high street shop front; or nattering to some bored farmer over a half-painted gate. I feel angry on behalf of the poor victim he's achieving so little for. I want to march up to him and give him a piece of my mind. But he's not my responsibility, so I hold myself back.

One could almost admire him for this dedication to demonstrating laziness. I don't. Anyone can be lazy. That man sets a bad example to the young men of this neighbourhood. He's a canker to the hard-working, businesslike, progressive values that the rest of us aspire to. Young men around here don't need anti-role models promoting sloth. It's hard enough to get the youth to apply themselves in the first place, without slovenly cretins like Chris flying the flag for low achievement. Chris is the antithesis of human endeavour and accomplishment. Our species stands for progression, movement, invention, advancement. Like it says in the Johnnie Walker adverts, we need to keep walking. Some people say I should leave him alone to get on and do his thing. Let him carry on in his sweet, unique way. Well, you could say that about a serial killer. It takes courage to promote decent values. And his way isn't sweet. It's annoying, irresponsible, inefficient and commercially unsustainable. I'm happy to bad-mouth him. I'll slag him off to any person who wants to mention him in conversation. I'll lambaste him at the bar, and I'll condemn him in the cafeteria. Proudly. He, on the other hand, has tried to talk to me many times. Connect. Conciliate. For the record, I'm neither interested in his life nor do I have the time to spare for his bullshit. Whenever he's tried to approach me, I've walked straight past. I won't be associated with that slothful, unskilled philanderer, even if he is my biological father.

ANGER MANAGEMENT

They'll be coming for me soon. They've detected signs of latent 'low level aggression' during the last five sessions. I can tell by their reactions. And because I've wanted to leave each session and punch a wall or kick a door or something. That shouldn't happen – not straight after a session. After a session I should be feeling my most virtuous. My most serene.

Five sessions should be enough to cure anything. In anyone. They don't publicly acknowledge the 'five session' rule. Everyone knows it exists. You only need a handful of examples of people disappearing after five sessions to figure it out. I feel angry – which isn't a good thing in my situation, admittedly – and annoyed. My annoyance is chiefly that a few years back, before The System was in place, someone displaying 'low level aggression' would have been perceived as normal. Before The System, I never picked a fight with another man; violently appropriated property; bullied; or vandalised anything of value. And I haven't changed. The System is the change. Because of it, I'm now one of society's most dangerous members. That's annoying to say the least. The System – so we're told – has turned habitual deviants into placid law-abiding citizens. It's replaced the need to capture and punish criminals. But that's only half the tale. Innocent people are still suffering; just in a different way. There is a new set of victims;

not of the aggression of others, but of The System. A process that was apparently created to protect us from deviants, has become the overbearing tyrant that diminishes our lives.

I'm no danger to mankind. All I want to do is bang or smash an inanimate object. Back in the day, all manner of upstanding individuals would participate in what is now categorised as low-level violence. It was an acceptable, dare I say, fun part of life. Shooting some tin cans lined-up on a derelict wall was a harmless way of letting off steam. The System doesn't seem able to distinguish between the desire to take part in that kind of activity and propensity for behaviour that is likely to have an negative impact on others. When I start thinking about the injustice of it all, my anger really kicks in. How ironic is that? A system designed to neutralise aggression, is fuelling it. My annoyance is exacerbated by the fact that The System seems to struggle more with 'low level aggression' than with extreme psychotic behaviour. It would seem that whilst it is able to detect aggressive tendencies, it is not able to quantify or categorise them. Compounding that, the treatment aspect it's heralded for, appears fundamentally flawed. It must have been developed to target and heal severely damaged parts of the brain. When it is presented with insignificant and impotent violent dispositions, that are perhaps distributed throughout the brain, it is unable to deactivate them. It is a crude sledgehammer trying to crack a nut. Mine on this occasion.

Don't get me wrong, it's brilliant for society that The System has eradicated practically all instances of murder, violent robbery and dangerous driving. But that is of no benefit to me. I am the new enemy. I am its victim. I have been singled out and will now be unable to enjoy the improved society that it has shaped. They're keen to keep reminding us how much better life is now. They constantly publicise the success of The System. They brag that, in three sessions, a previously dangerous member of society is made safe. Neutralised. If that's true, why has my desire to kick the odd mangy cat resisted continued treatment? Am I untreatable?

I finished my fifth session just over an hour ago. I've been home about twenty minutes. I came straight here. I knew I had to come here quickly. They won't lift you immediately after a fifth unsuccessful session – that would make make its failure all too obvious. They don't want the general public to know their grand design is defective. They'll give it an hour or two before they grab you. Just long enough to allow friends and family to imagine they've got you for something else, like spitting or dropping litter, but not so long that you'd have a real chance of escape. The 'give it a couple of hours' policy is both naive and patronising. If you suspect you've exhibited trace results, your associates soon know about it. Whether you talk about it or not, people will work it out. If you've been exiting sessions uncured, people can see it in your eyes; hear it in your voice. Worry and fear preoccupy you. You know you're being judged guilty by everyone and all the while failing to respond to the treatment prescribed to rehabilitate you. I've witnessed it in others and now I'm experiencing it for myself. It's like you're on Death Row but still roaming free; trying to get on with your normal life. You're hoping like hell that the parole board will realise you're not a bad person, but you know that the results from the character assessments are saying otherwise. The staff in the centres know you're failing. They're all sworn to secrecy, but there are so many people working in those places that word inevitably slips out. And The System isn't designed to weed-out gossips from society. It's designed to treat individuals with violent tendencies.

Once you've been grabbed, you are never seen again. I guess they kill System failures. Nobody knows. This provides me with two options: I wait around to be caught and slaughtered, or I can disappear. I don't want to vanish. I've got a great future. I had a great future. I'm still youngish. I haven't settled down yet. I'm intelligent. I've got an interesting job. I've got lots of friends. I'm deputy president of the local tennis table league. I don't deserve to disappear – not for five trace readings of 'low level aggression' – 'low level aggression' that ought to be easily extinguished by the very technology that detected it. But there's no point trying to argue. Getting agitated and angry is the very proof they're after. The threat I pose to society is scientifically proven as far as they're concerned. I'll go on the run. My chances aren't great out there on my own, but I'd rather have a slim chance than no chance at all. I'll look after myself. Answer to *my* agenda rather than theirs. I'll fish out my equipment from the old days; the camping gear, emergency medical kit, outdoor clothes, my knives. There are a couple of great knives under the floor of the shed – *really* great knives. Good for hunting. I can kill and butcher with those. I have killed and butchered with them. I'll take the rifle too; the rifle and plenty of ammunition. I've been hiding it all since they announced that The System was to be introduced. God I've missed using that stuff. I'll take the Glock too. Rifles can be great fun at distance, but you need something much more compact when you're operating at close quarters. I'll use the weapons primarily for hunting. But, if they try to take me in, I'll turn my killing skills on my pursuers. I'll revert to the ancient rule of kill or be killed – the law of The Jungle. I'm ready for The Jungle. The Jungle is the antithesis of the bland docility that The System represents. In The Jungle the strong and mighty rule. I'll take the Samurai sword too. Ammunition never runs out on that baby. Perfect for hunting. I used it on a prostitute before The System was introduced. First I fucked her. Then I beat her senseless. I used the sword on her as she crawled around pitifully on the floor, pathetically begging for mercy. I shoved the blade where my cock had just been. I hadn't initially intended to end her. But she would have grassed me up to the police for biting chunks of flesh from her tits as I pounded her. She said she wouldn't tell, but they always do. You can never trust a whore. Damn, it feels good to let it out; to admit it – I've killed before. I have killed! Yeah! Up until now I've been forced to pretend I'm totally uninterested in extreme violence. I managed to evade The System for years by suppressing my desires. But they improved The System to prevent the few premeditated crimes that were still occurring. The 'new and improved' System is obviously able to dig deeper into the psyche. I've been found out. I'm not bothered. In fact, I'm elated. The advanced technology is my saviour. Being discovered will be my rebirth. I am a killer who hasn't killed for over a decade. I've yearned for years to get my hands bloody again. The frustration has been unbearable. Now the wait is over. I feel thrilled. Invigorated. I'm excitedly running round my house and garden, getting ready to go rogue. I am reborn. I am gathering my tools together. I'm going to escape before they get here. I'm going to evade capture for the rest of my life. I'm going to carve again. I'm going to take the lives of others. For the first time in years, I'm going to feel the thrill of killing. And killing is the ultimate buzz. When you take another's life, you are their absolute master. For them, in that instant, you are God. I will be God again.

THE LAUGHTER BALLOON

The laughter balloon must never touch the ground. If it does, the population of the whole planet will perish. It was created by an exceptional scientist called Marcus. It is unlikely that there has been, or will ever be, another mind as brilliant as that of Marcus. Imagine someone with the inventiveness and aesthetic sensibilities of Leonardo da Vinci, the scientific and conceptual genius of Einstein, and the vision of Plato, living in the time of the Neanderthals. That was Marcus, compared to his contemporaries. Though I am compelled to describe him as a genius, the word seems a massive understatement.

The mechanism of the balloon is incredibly complex. Marcus designed it to remain airborne for eternity if necessary. I could go into great detail here; describing the advanced, self-sustaining, self-maintaining systems invented to prevent any attempts at interference and ensure the balloon's longevity; but the detail is inconsequential. It has been drifting aloft for twelve centuries now, and its still in perfect working order. But it is not the balloon that captures the public imagination. It is its payload. It carries a genocide-instigating cargo capable of annihilating the globally dispersed population within a few hours of its release. It might seem strange to discover, therefore, that, since he created this Armageddon device, Marcus has been universally adored.

Even his monstrous balloon is loved by its potential victims. I'll explain.

Marcus created the balloon because his civilisation was beginning to collapse. His people had reached an incredible level of scientific achievement. But they lacked all passion for life. Thanks to amazing medical advances, life expectancy was around six hundred years. As long as you didn't have an accident serious enough to kill you before help arrived; nothing would. There were no wars; there was no crime; you could take whatever drugs you wanted; there were no sexually transmitted diseases (and consequently everyone was fucking everyone); you could eat what you liked; you could be as lazy or as energetic as you wanted. Life was unbelievably easy. We all wish for the easy life. But even the easy life we dream of would still be full of immeasurably more concerns than Marcus's people faced. They all had incredibly, incredibly easy lives. But it wasn't doing them much good. Right about the time they solved the final part of the puzzle for maintaining extremely long life, they ran out of the passion for living it. I have to resort to French here to explain exactly what they lost – there's no English phrase that truly captures the essence of it: they lost their *joie de vivre*. For an individual, losing your verve can be debilitating. Joylessness is an attitude of mind that is hard to snap out of. It can ultimately lead to depression, self-harm or even suicide. When an entire species loses their joie de vivre, the only music left in their lives is a global mumbling funeral dirge as they shuffle off into extinction. If you find that hard to conceptualise; think of pandas. Pandas hate zoos. Knowing this, zoos go to incredible efforts to replicate their captive Pandas' indigenous surroundings. They give them interesting things to climb, they reproduce the temperature and humidity of a panda's natural environment. And they provide pandas with the correct food. Add all the elements together and you have a panda paradise. But pandas know it's fake. The black and white ursines are continually reminded of the reality of their phoney predicament by yellow, pink and brown faces staring at them through thickened glass. The cruelty of the deception sucks away their enthusiasm for life; their joie de vivre. Without this, they don't feel compelled to reproduce. Their numbers dwindle. Marcus's people were on that downward spiral. Everything had become fake because life itself was no longer real. Life was an artificially sustained state. The only way out was an instantaneously lethal accident or elective suicide (quite understandably, a legal right for a people set to endure six hundred-odd years of tedium). The number of births was at a historic low. Suicides were rising exponentially. Marcus's people were giving-up the ghost. There were pressure groups campaigning for radical solutions, but apathy amongst the population at large meant that each movement attracted few followers. These small collections of mildly motivated radicals failed to have any real impact on the self-destructive course of their species. What was needed was a single, gifted visionary who could devise and enact a master plan to reinvigorate the masses. Marcus was that man.

Marcus realised that nobody laughed any more. Laughter is all about the release of repression. We joke about things that we can't deal with. We make jokes about death, suffering, social and sexual inadequacy, cruelty and oppression. In Marcus's world, these things didn't exist. There was no death, no oppressive morality, no deprived minority. Medicine could award you any physical attributes you desired, all men and women were equal and nobody had any reason to be cruel. Marcus's solution was to create something that would bring the fear of death back into his fellow citizens' lives. He devised a virus so lethal, virulent and complex that it was completely incurable and would eradicate the entire species if released. This threat hanging over his people's heads would give them something to laugh about. The next phase was to create a mechanism that would deliver this genocidal menace into the daily lives of the populace. He realised that this needed to happen physically, tangibly, noticeably. The threat of something lethal hidden away in a vault somewhere wouldn't have the same psychological impact. So Marcus created the balloon.

The volume of gas in the balloon is regulated by a device that measures how much laughter is being emitted by the twenty thousand beings closest to it. If there isn't enough laughter, gas is released from the balloon and it starts to drop. When the laughter picks up, gas is injected and the balloon heads upwards. Directed by the wind, it floats around the planet, forcing those nearest to it to laugh. And it works. Fake laughter doesn't work. The instruments on board can detect the difference. Only true, heartfelt laughter makes the balloon fill up and rise. It's impossible to be empirical about how much laughter causes what degree of elevation. To be honest, I think the scale is purposefully elastic. All I can say is that when it is hovering above you, you make damned sure you find or create things to laugh at. When you consider the size of the population, the proportion of people who are at any one time responsible for sending it heavenwards, is relatively small. But since it is difficult to be precise about exactly who is being monitored, many more people make merry than need to. As the balloon moves around the sky, the responsibility to drive it upwards moves, sometimes slowly, sometimes quickly, from city to city, country to country. In anticipation of taking over joviality duties, those not under its influence closely monitor its whereabouts as it is tracked by satellite. Technical details of this report, along with the weather forecast (which focuses on wind direction), are the two most popular shows on television.

The nearest the balloon has ever come to colliding with earth or sea, is three thousand feet. That happened within a few decades of its release when a seemingly irreversible spiritual malaise had overcome the inhabitants of a specific geographical area. A series of enthusiasm-draining events had badly affected the community, making the local population lose interest in their own lives. When they saw the balloon above them, sinking ominously downwards, they were simultaneously gripped by the fear of mass mortality and a sense of responsibility for the continued existence of everyone on the planet. This jolted them into life and laughter. They sorted themselves out; managed to laugh despite everything – or nothing – and sent the balloon sky high. Marcus' genius was verified.

Everyone knows their duty. If you are working and the balloon floats into view, you cast aside your petty obsessions and start sucking the marrow out of life. Kids charge out of school and begin unrestrainedly enjoying themselves; sportsmen and women stop striving to win and remember the joy of just participating in their sport; even serious writers stop creating heavy material and start knocking out whimsical comedies. The greatest goal in this new and superior global society, is not creating new technology or furthering the boundaries of knowledge; it's sending the balloon higher than it has ever been. Under the balloon's overbearing presence, the populace throw themselves with such dedication at the business of having fun, that enjoyment becomes infectious. Many parties are so vibrantly intoxicating that they rage on for months after the balloon has breezed by.

Marcus is long dead. Although he was a genius beyond compare, there was one thing he was never able to do, and that was to be funny. He couldn't tell a decent joke to save his life. They say he never once made anyone laugh, or even crack a smile. He really was rather dull. This deficiency plagued him throughout his life, driving him repeatedly into deep despair. In fact, he struggled so terribly with depression that it was touch and go whether he'd manage to finish the balloon project. Dedication to the project was the only thing that had kept him going towards the end. Once he'd achieved his life's ambition, the awareness that he'd never be a fun person struck with irresistible force. Within a couple of hours of releasing his incredible airship unto the heavens, he took his own life.

CYRANO

There's a retired sniffer dog at the dogs' home. He's been there for ages. Nobody wants him. It's a shame. He was a brilliant sniffer dog who did great service to the community. He won three canine medals. His nose was so famous that the police called him Cyrano. At the dogs' home they've renamed him Jack. The voluntary staff there think it's an appropriate name for an ex member of CID – having watched far too many 1970s cop shows. I've always wondered why no one wants him. He's a retired hero after all. OK, he's got his faults – but haven't all dogs? He has no septum. That looks a bit odd, but dogs with worse physical imperfections have found homes. In the time that I've been going there, two three-legged dogs have gained new owners. It could be the tale behind his missing septum that's putting potential owners off. Or perhaps they're repulsed by his previous association with law enforcement organisations.

Jack was a plain-clothes specialist, working with the uniform brigade. He could sniff out all sorts of drugs with incredible accuracy at a remarkable range. But coke was his drug of choice. He was a cocaine specialist. That was cool with the coppers; they love getting hold of the stuff, and Jack could sniff out cocaine from twenty yards. Most sniffer dogs practically need their noses in a drug carrier's pocket to positively identify drugs. That makes them little more than a labour-saving device – saving the police the tedious business of having to carry out countless investigative searches. Jack was in a different league. He did the detective work for the cops. Jack would pick out the druggies as crowds shuffled past at railway stations, or indicate piles of belongings that needed special attention. If he signalled that someone was carrying, Jack's handlers would release him and he'd be onto cocaine sixty seconds before the Old Bill could catch up. In that time, Jack would rip out bags of cocaine from pockets and bags. In all the commotion of a public arrest, Jack would have had a few good snorts before the police intervened. They allowed this to happen. He was good because he wasn't just acting on training – he really wanted to find drugs. He needed to find drugs. Jack was an addict. Those first few sniffs were his reward for collaring a criminal. The police knew it was unethical, but he was great at his job. Jack's level of success reflected extremely well on the teams he worked with. And for them, letting a mutt grab a few nostrils full of white powder didn't seem too terrible a price to pay for their rocketing promotions. They wouldn't have let a human do the same, obviously.

Inevitably, like any addict, Jack ended up needing more and more of his drug to keep operating. He began to focus more on sucking it back than hunting it down. And, while he was buzzing, he was useless. At first the police were happy to let his detection rate drop off a little. But when it got so bad that it began affecting their bonuses, they realised they had to do something to keep Jack firing on all four paws. One of the policemen on the team had worked with addicts in an outreach centre. He recognised the signs of Jack's professional demise. The hound was prescribed with the very thing that a failing addict needs – regular fixes.

Every time they made a bust, ninety-eight percent of their cache was sent for incineration. The remaining two percent was used to keep Jack on track (with perhaps the odd bit being further siphoned off for big nights out for the squad). It got to the point where Jack was doing a gram in the morning just to get out of his kennel. He'd then do a whole shift, sniffing and snorting his way through around five busts a day. Finally, after many long hard hours at the snow face, they'd give him a few lines with his Pedigree Chum to keep him sweet.

Jack wasn't sleeping that well at the time. He lost his septum a few weeks before his eventual break-down. The disfigurement, combined with the increased inhalation capacity of his snout, may well have contributed to it. A police vet was called in to check Jack out. He was unaware of Jack's long history of drug dependency. His handlers insisted that the drug abuse was only happening during busts. This is what went in the vet's report. He was loyal to them, and to Jack's reputation. In truth, the clinical study found that the level of soft tissue corrosion in Jack's nasal passages indicated prolonged, systemic abuse.

Jack was retired with full honours, but he was in a mess. Before being sent to the dogs' home, he went through an eight week programme of treatment. The best way to effectively deal with an addiction is to replace it with another, less destructive addiction. For humans, religion or creative pursuits work well. These aren't options for canines. So they got Jack hooked on tea. Jack now goes through at least six pints of tea a day. That's a lot of liquid for a dog. At the dogs' home they have to be upfront about a pooch's needs. Any potential owners for Jack are informed that they'll have to provide him with lukewarm tea, in serious volume, from first thing in the morning to last thing at night. It is explained that if they don't keep him dosed-up on tea, he could have a relapse. That's quite a responsibility to take on.

Now that Jack's over his addiction, he behaves like every other reformed addict. He is fundamentally opposed to any sort of drug use. Even light pot smokers at the dogs' home have to give him a wide birth. He'd never attack anyone. He just creates the most terrible fuss when anyone with even the slightest whiff of drugs about them comes near him. Jack's cage at the home is at the end of a long corridor, and visitors are openly informed that he is an ex-sniffer dog who will begin the most frenetic barking if any drug user comes within twenty yards of his pen. Not a lot of visitors venture down that echoey hallway. Of those that do, some don't believe the staff's warnings. You should see their red, guilty faces when they hastily retreat from the barking drug alarm.

I don't do drugs. Perhaps you wonder why I don't take him on. Well, firstly I prefer Welsh Springer Spaniels – so I'm waiting for one of those to turn up – but, more importantly, I've got friends who might well take drugs. If they do, that's their business and I'd rather not know about it. If Jack lived with me, I'd know. It surprises me that no one has taken him though. I've always imagined a conservative mature couple who live in a quiet village somewhere would be attracted to his service record. The missing septum isn't such a serious disfigurement, and the tea drinking isn't an offensive habit (although he does need very regular trips to the garden). One day I asked the staff what stopped people taking him home; was it the missing septum, the tea addiction, the paramilitary record – or something else? It was something else, they said. No one loves a rat.

MIXED MEDIA

The paints used in my most celebrated work are mixed with human matter. It is a huge image on a massive canvas. It's eighteen feet wide and eleven feet high. It fills the end wall of the converted barn where I live alone. Several incredibly rich people have attempted to buy it. But it is the only work I have produced that I can guarantee you I will never sell. People look at it and say it inspires all sorts of emotions. I look at it and it inspires only one – fear. The fear of arrest and life imprisonment. Critics say it represents a tumultuous period in my artistic journey. They aren't too far from the truth. It emotionally, chronologically and physically represents the victory I had over my overbearing mentor. It both signifies, and is, the moment pupil mastered master.

Genius shines very early on in life. You can't always tell who might become a pretty good footballer, a decent musician or a wonderful dancer. Some seemingly gifted kids, like brilliant child actors, are flops as adults. Conversely, some rather good professional sportspeople take up sport far later in life than you'd imagine they'd need to. But genius shines from the very beginning. It glistens like a huge gold nugget in a pauper's worn-out, silt-filled prospecting pan. I am a genius painter. I am forty-seven and have been selling my art for thirty-four years.

My work first went on sale at an exhibition in the railway station in my town. My town was quite posh and you could trust the commuters to not vandalise or steal anything in the waiting room. Consequently, the waiting room, which was a throwback to the town's even more grand and affluent past, held biannual exhibitions featuring local artists. The station master was a retired butler who'd spent thirty years in the service of the Duke of Wessex. He treated the station with the same level of care that he'd treated the Duke's castle. Every single piece of brass on that station was as highly polished as the belt buckle of a Guardsman on royal duty. On a bright sunny day, metal surfaces around the station would gleam so brightly that its a wonder no traveller ever sued for permanent eye damage. Local people were incredibly proud of their station master, and their station. But the thing they liked most about their station was the six-monthly art show. Getting your work exhibited was a struggle for most. There were only places for six artists; each being allowed to display up to four works. There was physically enough space to show much more, but the station master had cultivated a fine sense of proportion for artistic display. To get your work included, you had to first show it to a panel of three judges. These judges – the station master, the Duke's son and our celebrated published lesbian poet – would, twice yearly, decide who was in and who wasn't.

When I was thirteen, I felt ready to test myself against the best talent in the area. Everyone except my mother advised me against it – amateur consultants because their minds weren't developed enough to recognise great work; my father because he wanted to protect me; and my school art teacher because he was jealous of my brilliance. I entered four pictures – four studies of a single tree. By that age I'd already amassed dozens of works. The trees were not the most popular of them with family and friends. But the studies showed something that I knew no other exhibitor in the area was capable of displaying; distinctive intelligent personal perspective combined with the talent to communicate it.

They went down a storm. There were so many offers for them, they ended up being sold by auction. The Duke of Wessex bought them. A couple of wealthy local businessmen bid for a while, but backed-out when the price didn't seem logical for the work of a thirteen-year old. The last pair bidding were the lesbian poet and the Duke. In the end, although she could see and appreciate my genius far more deeply than he could, he had more money. Old money. Those four pictures, which have since been inherited by the new Duke of Wessex, are the most valuable works in his long-accrued family collection.

Eight years later, at art school, I did a triptych of another tree. It was the tree that stood in the centre of a quadrant in our halls of residence. My aim was not to bring artistic insight to this lonely, over-pruned tree, but to impress a stunningly beautiful literature student. She had long, wavy dark hair, a Pre-Raphaelite face, teeth moulded from compressed moonbeams, the lips of a television advertisement lipstick model, the posture of a ballet dancer, the body of an It Girl, identical breasts to those of the young woman on my favourite soft-porn playing card from a pack I'd bought on a school-trip to France a handful of years earlier (the Queen of Diamonds), and a more awesome arse then that of the hottest lead dancer from Snoop Dog's raunchiest ever pop promo. We'd met by chance in an oldie-worldie pub. She told me that her favourite poet was the old lesbian back home. I lied saying that I was currently working on a project for her. I said I planned to sell it at a knock-down price in order to make up for her failure to secure my first sale. Over a glass of damson and greengage wine, we planned a trip back to my home town. In the following days I hurriedly bashed out 'Triple Tree'.

A week later we met up again and took a train to see that mature bird of letters. She met us at the station and drove us back to her house-plant littered, low ceilinged cottage. In front of the culture-vulture sex-kitten that was making us both drool, I offered Miss F. the exclusive opportunity to buy the trilogy. She bought it and I got laid. A lot. First time was on the way back to college in the toilets of the train station – which seemed apt. That was the last time I let any of my work go for anything other than an extortionate sum. You could say the old dear practically saw me coming.

Since my works go for an absolute fortune these days, I live an incredibly comfortable and luxurious lifestyle. I could easily stop painting altogether. I rarely create anything new any more. The only thing that drives me to occasionally produce new work now is boredom. I'm aware that that's a hollow reason for a genius artist to produce work, but it's the truth. Before I painted the massive canvass in this tale – which is officially entitled 'Storm' but I privately think of as 'Body' – I was prolific. Commentators (i.e. people who dedicate themselves to analysing me and my work but actually understand me far less than the landlady of the Mason's Arms) say that Storm represents the end of a traumatic search for my artistic soul. They say that the desire to get to that state propelled me to produce voluminous works. They believe that once I'd reached the pinnacle of self-knowledge, my fervour for exploration through artistic expression was gone. Now, so they all seem to believe, I have nothing to prove and the trickling flow of my artistic output is the naturally sluggish productivity of a peaceful soul. They couldn't be more wrong about what drove me to create so prolifically before Body.

In their efforts to comprehend my genius, 'experts' always allude to the fact that my mentor, Gervallus Domnor, went missing just before I produced Storm. They note that he went missing in a storm. They delight themselves postulating innumerable preposterous perspectives on that obvious connection. It's like watching five year-olds debate what makes the sun rise. Some claim it was Domnor's challenging influence that inspired me to work so hard before Storm, and that once he was gone, there was nothing left for me to respond to. Others suggest that my restricted output is a tribute to the missing great man; artistic retardation as an expression of mourning. Whilst art historians' opinions differ on what effect Domnor had on my earlier work and development, they all tend to agree that when he disappeared, I had a mental breakdown. I produced Body during that breakdown. They think it is the work of a madman. They are right. But they think the madness started when he went missing. They think his disappearance drove me into a state of severe depression. In that they are very wrong. What drove me under was Domnor himself. I was experiencing insane despair long before he vanished. Body doesn't represent a single period of intense emotional disturbance resulting from the loss of a friend. It marks the end game; the final phase of many long years of torturous oppression. It is the milestone that marks my escape from the abyss; my return to sanity. All their suppositions prove is the one eternal maxim: critics are generally wrong.

Here's a tip when it comes to appreciating contemporary art:

judge for yourself which works are great and which are rubbish. If you think a graffiti artist's spraying is great; stand by your opinion. Truly great works will eventually proclaim themselves - it's just a matter of a little time and exposure. If particular contemporary artists do need to be heralded as outstanding, then such demarcation should be the sole responsibility of vibrant creative thinkers – individuals almost capable of creating timeless masterpieces themselves. It isn't. This process is policed by elderly conservative art professors; old duffers whose thoughts and references are firmly rooted in the past.

The reason this bothers me is that when I was a fragile virtuoso in need of canonic accreditation, I got nothing. That's when I realised that critics behave like herd animals. They are so afraid of the consequences of putting a foot out of line that they slavishly follow the acknowledged leaders. When Domnor was still alive, not one critic dared hail my absolute genius; risked suggesting that I was the greatest living artist. And those that had the courage to mention my brilliance would either reference him or you could easily detect his spectre in their words. Consequently, his overbearing influence coloured the world's view of my work. Whereas articles about him, if references were needed, would never mention me. They would cite timeless masters like Monet, Van Gogh, Rothko or Vettriano. But, much as the critics pissed me off, the thing that *really* bothered me was the man himself.

We first met when I was at art college. The lecturers there realised there was nothing they could teach me so they contacted him. Domnor. They probably expected a response from him of no more than a few words of advice and a handful of brief pithy critiques. What happened was completely unexpected. Domnor invited me to join him at his studio. No other artist had ever received this awesome opportunity. It was a bewildering recognition from a man who, at that time, I thought was an exceptional individual. I worked at his studio, under his wing, for five years. Those five years were the most intense of my entire life. I was pushed, challenged, questioned, taught, lectured, ignored, ridiculed, tormented and driven. I hated every moment. The one thing that kept me there, in the face of incredible and relentless pressure, was the belief that one day he'd start to recognise my brilliance and cherish me. He didn't. After five years, driven to the point of despair and beyond, I left. I was established by then, and thought that leaving was the step I needed to take to become the master of my own artistic destiny. I thought that within a year or two of working in isolation, further developing and refining my own style, Domnor would begin to respect my genius. He didn't.

After I'd gone my separate way, on the few occasions when we'd meet, he'd be even more vitriolic. He'd attack my work (which was selling for millions) as juvenile and under-developed. He'd tear into me for my decision to leave his studio. He told me I lacked the discipline and maturity to go it alone. He cited his own personal history; saying he'd studied under the wing of another great artist until he was well into his thirties. He called me arrogant, flawed, stilted, rough. Fed up with his constant condemnation, I decided to sever all connections. I moved to Barcelona, where many of the world's elite artists were congregating at the time. I hoped to find some brotherhood and inspiration there. I did. Other artists and the Spanish critics were incredibly positive about the influence Spain and the creative milieu had on my work. Domnor wasn't, and the distance didn't silence him. It had the opposite effect. No longer able to chastise me face to face, his criticism became more public. He kept up with my creations from afar; savaging them, criticising my new lifestyle and belittling the influence of those he regarded as lesser artists. I detested his washing of dirty canvasses in public. The constant questioning of my ability, from the world's other most respected living artist, was more than I could bear. I had just about managed to cope with his private sneering at close quarters. Once it seemed to be influencing the opinions of the wider art establishment, I broke. It was at this point that I went mad and decided to kill him.

Most people think of homicidal madness as an insuppressible desire which drives immediate action, regardless of the consequences. Madness can actually inspire incredible levels of control and lucidity, during which the would-be murderer flamencos with immoral and irrational cravings. Although I had decided to end Domnor's life, I realised that if I'd killed him then, I would have been the prime suspect. I had motive. Rushing into the act would have also increased the likelihood that I'd generate evidence. Living so far away, no longer part of Domnor's life and routine, I was more inclined to make behavioural presumptions that would lead to executional errors (if you'll excuse the pun). I wanted him dead but I didn't want to go down with him. I wanted to be the unpunished vanquisher.

One thing I *did* know, one constant that ran throughout his life from schoolboy to septuagenarian, was that he loved sailing racing dinghies. He had not let age diminish him. He was a tough old guy who loved a challenge. He would still take his little dinghy out in rough weather. This would be the key to his undoing. I based my murderous plan on that knowledge.

I stayed in Spain for another eighteen months after deciding to assassinate him. In that time, I turned my attention to the subject of ancient maritime artefacts. Critics surmised that I was exploring the roots of my mentor's passion; seafaring. This association fortified my intentions. Everything I did while he was alive would be related to him. It had to end. He had to end. I was using the whole nautical enterprise as a facade. I wanted to learn how to scuba dive. I dived on ancient wrecks, and in order to maintain the deceit, produced sculptures and paintings inspired by the finds. My work appealed to a new cadre of customers; wealthy yacht owners. Because of this, it started achieving even greater premiums at auction. When I was a competent enough diver I returned home. By that time, Domnor had moved to a studio on the coast. He was enjoying life; sailing as much as he was painting. Any spare time not taken up by these two pursuits, he dedicated to assaulting me via the art world and the press.

On returning to my homeland, I befriended a withering teacher from art school. I didn't particularly like him, but he worshipped me and my work. He also knew Domnor, whom he admired even more. Because he knew us both, he was tortured by the bitter dynamic that existed between us. Predictably, he seized on the opportunity to engineer a reconciliatory meeting with Domnor. I feigned resistance for months. Eventually, externally reluctant and internally jubilant, I accepted.

I met Domnor at his studio. He was his usual bitter self. He kept ranting on about finding no possible reason for my move into ancient maritime imagery. He felt it was completely arbitrary – the random selection of a madman. For once, apart from the randomness of my subject matter, he was right. He'd find out the reason soon enough. I broke down in front of my tormentor.

The art school don left us alone. Domnor was an incredible judge of artistic truth, but an appalling judge of acting. He swallowed my performance hook, line and sinker. Engendering his sympathy meant phase two of my unwell mind's plan was accomplished. Phase three's objective was to induce him to invite me to come back to live with him again; to nestle back under the wing that purportedly nurtured and sheltered the vulnerable fledgling. Phase four of the plan was to kill him. Phase five – to paint a picture utilising his blood and liquefied body tissue – evolved organically.

I moved in, and endured two more years of claustrophobic chastisement before I felt I'd be beyond reasonable suspicion for his murder. He drove me so crazy during those two years that I am amazed I retained enough composure to carry out such a clinical operation. But my goal was so incredibly important that I managed to stay the course. The only thing that enabled me to continue functioning during that period was intense immersion in my work. It was important that both my behaviour and output showed no signs of the frustration and anger I was feeling. I couldn't telegraph my hatred. I had to appear motiveless. The constant suppression of emotion and desire caused me horrendous inner turmoil, and the need to express myself without giving the game away resulted in a fierce, distorted creative drive. Over those twenty-four months I produced the most exciting and vibrant body of work that I ever have or will.

After two years I was ready to complete my plan. If I'd left it much longer, I would have been the dead one. There were staff to look after us, but none lived at the studio. The nearest living soul was a crab fisherman two miles up the coast. It was Easter, and Domnor, a slave to tradition, gave his staff the long weekend off. They went home. We were left to eat pre-prepared meals and clear the tables ourselves afterwards. We did little of either, preferring to half starve in a creative dump every Easter and Christmas. On Easter Sunday, my dreams were answered. A minor storm kicked-up and Domnor headed out to sea in his dinghy. I donned my scuba gear and finned out to join him. It caught him completely off guard when I broke the surface, grabbed the side of his pathetic little boat, and capsized it. He'd always spouted that I was incapable of surprising him. It was delightful, therefore, to witness his stunned, horrified expression as I grabbed him by the hair and dragged him under the frothy waves.

He was getting old, and the shock of immersion in cold water rendered him virtually powerless. He was wearing his life jacket, but I clung hard to his long, sodden, greasy, grey hair with both hands and finned downwards, guffawing out bubbles as he gasped salt water into his lungs. Above the surface, his skinny legs kicked uselessly, waggling like those of a duck that's bobbed underwater to feed and had its neck clamped in the jaws of a fifty-pound pike. As blue-green brine filled his lungs, his eyes at last admitted how wrong he'd been about me – I was his superior.

When he stopped squirming, I calmly unfastened his lifejacket and let it drift away. I knew he had a reputation for regularly refusing to wear it. This kind of in-depth personal knowledge of your victim is the key to a perfect murder. I imagine I looked like an otter with a limpet-bashing pebble on its stomach as I swam on my back, cradling Domnor's limp body, all the way to my anchor point. As part of my 'marine' phase, I'd studying anchors and had had loads delivered to the boatshed-cum-studio at the far end of the cobbled yard. No inventory of the angular chunks of metal was kept. I'd built a nest of them on the sea bed half a

179

mile from our studio. When I reached the stack of anchors, I expertly secured my former mentor's corpse to it with chains and ropes. Advanced scuba diving courses have several benefits. Excellent knot-tying skills is one of them. Then I drained the blood from Domnor's body using a stock of heavy-gauge hypodermic needles and syringes. The most memorable image of the harvesting was the blood that seeped out from each pin-head-sized puncture wound as I pulled the loaded syringes out of his pale, wrinkled, liver-spotted neck. On a couple of occasions I stared in frozen fascination at ribbon-like streams of little red blobs marching away from his cadaver in slow-motion procession. I didn't think I'd ever admit this, but I might as well, seeing as I'm telling you everything: I masturbated at one stage while watching blood hypnotically emanating from a perfect puncture wound that sunk directly into his carotid artery. And wanking in a wetsuit, in dark, chilled North Sea waters, isn't easy. When he was finally empty, I zipped him up in a body bag, stashing the sealed blood cartridges inside, and swam back to dry land.

At ten O'clock that night, I alerted the coast guard. At one in the afternoon the next day, they found his boat smashed up on some rocks three miles to the south of our studio home. A week later, his unfastened lifejacket was found by two kids playing truant; washed-up on an amber-hunter's beach. I was never more than casually questioned. The ill-educated police seemed to think that because I am an incredibly intelligent man - an artistic genius - I couldn't be a killer. Thank goodness for the intellectual inferiority complex of those who've undergone state education!

I laid off the staff after he died. No one questioned my motives. Mourning is a fabulous excuse for unpredictable behaviour, which makes the death of a close friend or relative remarkably enabling.

After a couple of weeks, I retrieved the blood and kept it, for convenience, in the wine fridge. I waited until three months after the funeral before recovering Gervallus' body. He was still in relatively good shape; the body bag had prevented sea creatures from eating him and the cold sea water had helped preserve his decrepit form. I sawed his body into manageable pieces and kept them in the large freezer in the cellar. When the supply of blood had run dry and I needed more matter to mix with the paints for Body, I'd defrost these portions, remove the bones, and liquidise what remained. The resultant material mixed remarkably well with paint, giving it a three dimensional quality that adds depth to the canvas.

Unsurprisingly, Storm (or Body) depicts a storm. A raging storm forcing my lifelong motif – trees – to bend and cower in every possible direction. This is a wilful storm. It *knowingly* forces itself upon the subjugated flora. This storm has, according to a few remarkably astute critics, a mind of its own. For once, they are right – although they'll never know the full accuracy of their assessment. Because the heart of the storm does have a mind of its own – Domnor's. I have blended his pureed brain into the greys and purples that form the tempest's epicentre. His mind controls and directs the raging weather system. The grey matter that drove me into insanity drives the winds that dominate the massive canvass. With regards to the fate of Domnor's other vital organs, his liquefied heart is now set hard in the shadow of the only undisturbed object in the image – the mountain. I am the mountain. The mountain is the only part of the image that contains no element of him. I stand proud of him. His heart is in my shadow. At last, he is in my shadow. He is my shadow and my victim. I own him. His body is splattered across my most revered creation. Every last bit of it except for his eyes – his most prized sensors; the things through which he saw my work. They didn't deserve to be part of my greatest achievement. I ate them with some scrambled duck eggs and toasted rye bread the day after I'd fished him out of the sea. I had to cook them for quite a while because they'd been sat in his dead head for weeks, and I didn't want to let him poison me after his death. Consequently they were rubbery and the seawater had turned them very salty. This made them a bit hard to swallow, but I managed it. I kept them down, so they couldn't have been that bad.

I'll never sell Storm. Never. It means far too much to me. It marks my triumph over my tormentor. It represents the moment my tortured slave was set free. And, on a more practical level, it contains enough forensic evidence to get me banged-up for life.

CREAM

Terry said he couldn't eat cream. He could eat cream. He liked cream. In fact, he loved cream. He was on his first date with Rachael. They'd bumped into one another at a wedding three weeks earlier; both escaping a heaving hotel dance floor to suck in some late-night city air. She was breathtakingly beautiful – far too attractive for someone like him. They were the sort of couple that if you saw them together, you'd instantly wonder what a girl like her was doing with a guy like him. Men would presume he was either rich or had a huge dick. Women would think he was either rich or great fun to be with (well, at least that's what women would openly admit to thinking). Terry wasn't rich. He wasn't one of the funniest men around. He was far from charismatic. And his penis was sort of average. But, as they'd stared, together, at the illuminated cityscape beyond the bustling single-wedding-guest-meat-market, he'd plucked-up the courage to ask Rachael out. That made Terry a little bit special. Most men wouldn't dare to try it on with Rachael – not even after a few confidence-enhancing drinks.

Back to their first date. Stunning Rachael and ordinary-at-best Terry were having dinner. The meal had been going well, with wine and conversation both flowing freely. Things had been going so well, in fact, that despite his social and his aesthetic weaknesses, Terry seemed to be, in old-fashioned terminology, 'on a promise'. You could sense the frisson from about halfway through the main course. Then came dessert. Rachael chose *tarte au citron*. Terry opted for sticky toffee pudding. Once they'd made their revealing selections, the bubbly waitress delivered some bad news. She explained that they usually offer cream with all deserts. But the milkman hadn't turned up that morning because of a family crisis. The restaurant had gone on to receive more diners than usual, and the cream had nearly run out. There was only enough left for one portion. Rachael, as good-natured as she was good-looking, immediately offered Terry the cream. She said that she'd just as happily eat her dessert without. This presented Terry with a huge dilemma. He appeared to have two options: say no to Rachael's offer and insist she had the cream, or accept her generous gesture. Saying no might seem the gentlemanly thing to do, but it was fraught with negative connotations. He got the impression from Rachael that she was pretty emancipated and would not appreciate such antiquated gender differentiation. Refusing the offer might give her the impression that he subscribed to an outdated etiquette which she rejected and despised. However, he might have read her politics wrong. Though subscribing to some ideal of equality, she may have only made the offer out of courtesy; secretly desiring the cream for herself. If he took the cream, she might resent watching every mouthful of cream-coated sticky toffee pudding that he shovelled into his mouth. That would piss on his bonfire. Terry was facing one of those horrible stomach-cramping moments in life when you're offered two options, both of which suck. He did what any intelligent sexually-inspired human in charge of their own destiny would do. He crafted a third option. He flipped the coin and made it land on its side. "I'm actually allergic to cream Rachael," he said, with an Oscar-grade sprinkling of sincerity and embarrassment. Terry's dishonest revelation took the date to a whole new level – 'on a promise' became 'On. I promise'. His masterful display of vulnerability appealed to Rachael. It brought out her caring side. That, combined with the fact that she would now enjoy a healthy serving of cream with her *tarte au citron*, was a psychological and sensory knock-out punch. She was bowled over. Terry was food for her hungry soul. He was a raw steak dropped into a her piranha pool. From that moment on, she was all over him like the cream all over her lemony pudding. She began tucking in. It was sweet and sharp with creamy edges. Her taste buds were ignited and instantly quenched with every mouthful. She was the cat that got the cream. You could almost detect light purring as she exhaled between morsels. Terry's apparent allergy absolved her of guilt, right down to the last lick of her spoon. After desert they had coffees – hers white, his black. Terry hated black coffee.

Terry drove Rachael home. On the way, she asked him if his allergy was so serious that he couldn't kiss someone who'd recently eaten cream. After a long pause of fear and excitement, he calmly explained that his allergy wasn't that extreme. He just couldn't ingest dairy products. He said they upset his stomach rather than caused anaphylactic shock. He couldn't hold milk-derived substances down and would be horrendously sick if he consumed any. He winced as he told her, worrying that the detail might turn her off. But by then she was eating out of Terry's hand. His words were the sweetest love poetry she'd ever heard. They shagged on their first date; something neither of them had ever done before. Rachael because she'd never had to, and Terry because he'd never had the chance to. In the morning, after a shower, Rachael gave Terry his first ever tit-wank. He fell deeply in love.

Under Rachael's influence, Terry smartened-up his act. He got a trendy haircut; Rachael went with him to the hairdressers – her hairdressers. He started going to the gym. His old wardrobe was gradually phased out. He lost his air of desperation. He changed so much that other women started noticing him; commenting that they could *almost* see what Rachael saw in him. What really fascinated them though, was why she'd bothered in the first place. They concluded that she was either sensitive and strong enough to respond to some kind of inner beauty in him, pursuing it regardless of the disapproval of others, or that she was completely incapable of holding on to a decent man. Either way, to all the women who'd once been jealous of Rachael, she was no longer the enemy. Conversely, men became less interested in her. Nothing dampens a predatory male's ardour more than seeing the object of his attention with a nerd. They resort, as previously mentioned, to the old failsafe of believing that this guy's secret must be tucked away in his trousers. And if she's happy to hang round with a loser for that and that alone, then she isn't worth bothering about. Although this belief helped male observers rationalise the mismatched relationship, it also made them feel incredibly uncomfortable. The idea that there might be a geek at a party with a bigger dick than theirs, seriously undermined their fragile egos. Their puzzled frowns were as easy to read as neon signs at night, and their noticeable distress tickled the sisterhood. Theories and counter theories resounded. All in all, Terry and Rachael became everyone's private entertainment.

Rachael didn't care what others thought. She was just happy.

She had wasted far too much time on well regarded suitors who all turned out to be tossers. Not one of them had ever made her deep-down happy. Terry did. Aside from the appearance imbalance, they were a really good couple. Rachael, often categorised simply by her appearance, was actually an interesting, multi-faceted individual. She needed and deserved an interesting partner. Terry was that. He was quirky and engaging. Despite appearances, they were made for each other. But both found people's constant fascination with their pairing extremely wearing. They felt like the leading exhibit at a Victorian freak show.

A year after Terry had falsely claimed he was allergic to dairy produce, he and Rachael arrived in Bali for an eight-week backpacking holiday around South East Asia. Both had been keen to avoid the main tourist trails and half way into their expedition, they found themselves on a little rough-and-ready cargo boat bound for a remote island. They were in heaven – truly enjoying one another's company, without a single curious, judgemental tourist in sight. Thai people didn't scrutinise them and try to analyse what they were about. They weren't intrigued as to why such a good-looking woman would be with such an unattractive man. Perhaps they had different aesthetics. Perhaps they didn't particularly care about the personal lives of Westerners. Or perhaps they were just happy getting on with their own lives. Ten and a half hours into the voyage, as the day grew to a close, they were caught in a terrible storm. The crew fought desperately to prevent their profit-maker capsizing; constantly changing course in hopes of outrunning the teeth of the typhoon. They managed to stay afloat for two unchartered days before the storm finally got the better of them. A monster wave picked their rustic vessel out of the ocean and flung it violently onto an outcrop of cold, uncaring rocks. It was smashed apart. Fortunately, that brutal outcrop was just off the shore of an uninhabited island, and, with considerable effort, they all struggled to the safety of the drenched sandy beach.

Though the boat was trashed beyond any hope of repair, they managed to salvage nearly all of what was on her. They retrieved a couple of days worth of regular rations; materials to make a decent shelter; bedding and the cargo. That cargo would provide a far greater challenge to Terry and Rachael's future than their waitress's revelation had a little over a year earlier. That little ship had been carrying dairy products to inhabited islands too small to support herds of cattle or goats. There were gallons upon gallons of long life milk; tins of processed cheese; crates of evaporated milk; tubes of instant whipped cream; ready-mixed scrambled egg containing milk and butter; tins of macaroni cheese; boxes of rice pudding; and cartons of custard. Pretty much anything and everything made from or inseparable from dairy produce, was on that boat. It wasn't easy explaining Terry's allergy to the crew. By the time the message had sunk in, there was very little of the regular rations left. Soon the cargo was all that remained to sustain them. There was nothing edible living or growing on their isolated island, and they had nothing to fish with. Terry was again confronted with a milk-produce-centric dilemma. It took him right back to that moment between the main course and dessert on his first date with Rachael. Yet again, it seemed there were only two choices. He could admit to the love of his life; the woman who had made his life worth living, that he wasn't really allergic to dairy. Or he could starve. This time around, he couldn't come up with a third option. Admitting the truth would have undone the very knot that had bound their fates together.

It would have meant telling Rachael that the seed that grew into their beautiful flowering love was a poisonous spore. It would corrupt everything that had followed. If Rachael found out that his allergy was a lie, what could she believe? Everything about their relationship would be brought into question. Lies are invisible contamination. Once you're aware of lies, you can't work out what they've touched. Terry knew that. Rachael and he had often talked about how much they hated lies, and how destructive they were. There seemed no credible third way. Terry chose to starve.

The first two weeks were the hardest. Watching Rachael and the crew feast on sweet smelling rice pudding or sizzling scrambled eggs, was physical and mental torture. Initially, Terry's stomach grumbled with criticism, then it ached with despair. Eventually, it cramped and clawed at his insides like a nest of starving rats trapped under an upturned ceramic bowl on his belly, attempting to gnaw and scratch their escape through his abdomen. After two weeks of starvation, he still felt pain but it was more of a distant awareness, as his beleaguered brain increasingly lost interest in processing it. He became weak and lethargic. Eventually, all he could do was lie, helplessly, in the shelter the others had built for him, which overlooked the beach. His body slowly consumed his fat reserves. Then his internal organs. As he imploded, his mind would zone in and out of lucidity. Pain, hunger, regret, pride, joy, amusement, and then, again, pain would wash over him like the waves he gazed blurrily out at. Time lost its meaning. It was a like being on an unending magic mushroom trip. He knew when death was closing in on him. He'd drift seamlessly in and out of consciousness. He'd be wide awake for hours at night, then asleep during long chunks of the hot, humid days. Rachael tried to bring some normality to his unmarked hours. She'd tell him what time and what day of the week it was, or that they'd soon be rescued, or just talk to him about the fun times they'd had together.

On the day of his death, her behaviour changed. They both sensed he was going. They were in perfect tune with one another – Terry's one lactic lie excepted. Staring death in the face caused Rachael to drop her pretence that everything was going to be alright. All morning and afternoon she sat at his side, stroking his face and hair. The last time his eyes opened, through failing hazy vision, he watched a tear escape her eye and gradually make its way down her sculpted cheek. Sensing his near departure, she leant over him, and that warm single tear dropped away from her face. To Terry, it seemed to hang in the air for hours, glistening like a diamond. Then it landed on his cracked bottom lip, and gently trickled into his mouth.

His last living taste was distilled suffering. It was condensed emotion. It was ambrosia drawn up from her heart. But most importantly of all, it was honest – the well-seasoned honesty of loss. It was a drop of true love – love that he'd savoured; love he'd consumed voraciously. The deep felt love that only exists between two people who keep nothing from one another. It was a drop of salty water ten thousand times more delicious than a serving of fresh cream. He stared at his fiancée and knew he'd made the right decision to starve.

Rachel and the stranded sailors buried his emaciated corpse on the far side of the small island. Two days later, they were rescued.

JULIAN'S BOAT

Julian had a lifelong dream to build the longest ever wooden boat. He came from a family of boat builders. His dad owned a boat-yard that he'd inherited from his father who in turn had inherited it from his father. The family claimed they could trace involvement in boat building back to the construction of Sir Frances Drake's fleet. I never saw the evidence. Whatever the truth of the matter, boat building has certainly been a significant part of their family history. Julian's great-grandfather designed a boat used by whalers. It was such an impressive vessel, that at one stage half the North Atlantic's whaling fleet was made up of them. Julian's granddad created a vessel so robust that it became the universal preference of lifeboat organisations the world over. And with the highly desirable pleasure craft his father built, he literally ruled the waves in the leisure market. This impressive track record presented Julian with two things: the wealth to build the longest ever wooden boat and the desire to be as renowned and respected in the boat world as his male predecessors.

Julian was an incredibly imaginative designer. His nautical originality was truly inspirational and surpassed even that of his gifted ancestors. His design for the world's longest ever vessel was his dissertation. It earned him a first class degree in ship-building. After leaving university, he spent five years collecting the timber he needed for his ambitious project. He needed a huge stock of long, strong timbers, and travelled from country to country buying at specialist auctions. Getting hold of the raw materials was less than half the trouble. Constructing the craft was by far the bigger challenge. It was one hell of a job, and it absorbed the efforts of up to two thirds of his father's skilled workforce. Although he relied upon his doting father's sponsorship, the scale and ambition of the project brought him much attention and praise. Julian became a boating celebrity well before his baby was ready to set sail.

Eventually, even the mightiest projects reach a conclusion. After three years hard toil, and no little expense, Julian's vessel was ship-shape. Since his dream was to create the world's longest boat – a record-breaker – proportionate width was never a priority. Cost and materials put further pressure on her girth. She was, therefore, only fifteen metres wide at her slender mid-point. And since she was one hundred and sixteen metres long, she had a very different shape to most ocean-going vessels. Even to the casual observer, she looked relatively narrow. But this was always going to be the case. And she was a special ship. An elegant, world-beating achievement. She cut a striking dash.

When the day of the launch came and the ship received her champagne christening, her beautiful viewing galleries and decadently carved bars thronged with the great and good of the maritime world. As she slipped elegantly out to sea, her noble streamline form slicing through the waves like a slender wooden dolphin, the roar of the cheering crowds and the triumphant swell of an enthusiastic brass band on the dock intermingled in a celebratory cacophony that rushed out to meet the sound of the waves. The billowing sails swelled like party balloons, and the graceful vessel rapidly picked up pace. In thrilled reaction to the dynamic forward surge, the applause of the crowds aboard and on land rose. Captain Julian stood, at the helm, proud and fulfilled, his face beaming like a lighthouse. He had done more than match the achievements of his forebears – he had exceeded them. As they sped gloriously onwards, the harbour and jubilant landlubbers fast disappearing behind them, he took masterful command of his impressive vessel, turning the magnificent wheel to steer her into the setting sun and towards her first port of call.

And she snapped in half. God, she was a glorious sight to behold. A wonderful looking, beautifully finished, world-record breaking craft. But she wasn't half skinny and she was never going to survive that turn.

FEELING MYSELF
PART II

After a frustrating day spent trying to figure out how I came to be covered in impregnable skin, I retired to my still-smelling-of-Melanie bed with the intention of repeating the previous night's wankathon. But my desire for masturbatory escapism was not sated. Everything felt different. Despite well-practised methods, I could not stimulate myself. This made me even more anxious that the real me was slipping further from my grasp. Sexual and cerebral frustration levels grew so unbearable that I felt like cutting my wrists. But I'd tried that with a Stanley Knife earlier in the day and failed miserably. Eventually, exasperated and exhausted, I passed out.

I woke surrounded by a gaggle of white-uniformed attendants, mouth-masked like bleached highwaymen. And I was no longer at home, having been transported to what appeared to be an operating theatre overly-equipped with bright spotlights all pointed directly at me. If it wasn't for a proliferation of the type of medical equipment you'd see in a TV hospital drama, the shocks of unkempt human hair contained in flimsy surgical hats, and the many pairs of busy hands tightly wrapped in cloudy latex gloves, I'd have imagined I'd been abducted by aliens. Not that seeing recognisably human forms brought any comfort. I had been kidnapped and my terrestrial abductors were fussing around me like worker bees attending to their Queen. My immediate reaction was to sit up, but when I attempted to do so, my forehead smacked against what I presumed was a sheet of electrified reinforced glass just above it. And fuck it hurt. With a run-up no longer than the width of my septum, it felt like I'd had a set-to-linen electric iron slammed violently against the front of my skull. A pitiful groan escaped from my mouth and I lay back down, adopting a state of elective paralysis in order to avoid further agony. But my yelp energised the mouth-masked attendants, as if an Asian Giant Hornet had invaded their hive and was approaching their Queen. It set one racing towards me, its sting at the ready – a primed syringe. Petrified, all I dared move was my eyeballs, which felt as if they'd gone into spasm as I tried to take in as much of the scene as possible without moving a muscle. But I was unable to maintain my static state. As the needle closed in on my right eyeball, my arms instinctively sprung up to intercept. Big mistake. Every bit of my body that moved sizzled with sickening agony. My hands, arms and shoulders felt like they were being flayed with turbine-mounted chains of broken-glass-studded jellyfish tentacles rotating at five thousand revolutions per minute. I collapsed into rigid submission, and the rapidly homing-in needle was inserted into me just above my right tear duct; an Achilles Heel my previous day's experimentation had failed to find.

It was all Dad's fault.

Dad made his money buying and selling. He started as a schoolboy, getting free sacks of out-of-date monkey nuts from his aunt's health food shop, roasting them in the family oven for free, and delivering them in the evenings, by bike, to townsfolk with the munchies. This was a profitable business in an era before twenty-four hour garages, particularly when your expenditure level is practically zero. His earnings were so high that he had to complete a tax return at fourteen – deducting the purchase price of his bicycle as a work expense, of course. He ended up buying and selling companies so large that it was joked he had enough liquidity to trade in minor nations. But, despite all his business success, the only natural child he produced (me) suffered from a debilitating genetic disorder. I was born with acute Epidermolysis Bullosa. My skin was so sensitive that it would blister and fall off at the slightest touch. Had the severity of my condition been only slightly worse, my entire skin covering would have been stripped off me as I emerged from the vaginal passage – my mother's own birth canal serving as lethal torture chamber. That level of injury would have been terminal, even with the backing of Dad's once phenomenal wealth.

They call kids born with this condition Butterfly Children, because our skin is as fragile as a butterfly's wings. Have you ever touched a butterfly's wings? The gentlest of prods will leave your fingertip coated in a guilty dusting of multicoloured scales fine as talcum powder. The butterfly suffers for your fingertip makeover – it is left with an oval wound on its wings that is, at best, an area where its colourful patterns have been crudely smudged and, at worst, a gaping hole crossed with feeble remnants of it's branch-like wing skeleton. I went to a butterfly exhibition once, where children were encouraged to get close to living butterflies. These living exhibits were no common or garden butterflies; they were spectacular primeval flying insects, giant garishly coloured ones fluttering around an uncomfortably humid greenhouse crammed with flappy-leaved plants, plates of fast-rotting fruit and lots of kids - mostly quite small ones for whom the largest butterflies must have looked like camp eagles. As I went in, the first thing that hit me was the chest-slap of instant immersion into high humidity – like stepping off an air conditioned aeroplane in the tropics. Next came the sickly-sweet smell of fruit offerings for the butterflies to lick – which confused me because I'd always thought butterflies drank nectar. Then came the noise of the children. It wasn't a recognisable group of children sound – like playground kids, party kids, amusement park ride kids or swimming pool kids – and it was this difference, the newness of this chorus that struck me. I was immersed in a soundscape of childish awe and wonderment. When I first stepped into that sound, its originality convinced me that it would be the most enduring memory of my Butterfly World visit. It wasn't. Seeing the results of repeated tiny-fingertip abuse to once-graceful butterflies stripped of the power of flight, is what stayed with me. There were signs everywhere telling the beauty-struck children not to touch. But half were too young to read, and the other half were so bedazzled they ignored the instruction. I heard a guide warning a group of children that touching the wings would burn them. I don't know if that's the official term for describing the wing damage, but it certainly fitted the injuries. The worst affected insects looked like they'd had their wings held open by gnarled pliers while a medieval torturer sizzled through them with a red hot poker. My skin was that delicate once. I'd forgotten all about it though, thanks to a programme of repressive hypnotism ordered by my father. Apparently he insisted it was 'for the best' and 'for my own good'. It's much more likely that it was for him – to make his life easier; to help him forget the truth about me.

My entire body is swathed in moistened elasticated bandages, there are drips in both my arms, and I am lying on a tailor-made, super-soft-rubber-mattressed hospital bed at the heart of The Sanctuary. And while I've been lying here, scared and bewildered, my peculiar nature has been revealed by loose-tongued medical staff. On top of what I've gleaned from their idle chatter, each careless slip of the tongue has triggered the release of suppressed memories – allowing them to flutter to the surface. I've gathered those snippets and memories in a net, and crushed them together to form a mosaic picture of who I am. I spent the first seven years of my life imprisoned here, with some of the most brilliant doctors and nurses on the planet keeping me dosed-up on painkillers and treating my injuries while the world's best geneticists worked day and night to develop a cure. But as is often the case, a cure was far more elusive than a fix. Jenner didn't cure smallpox, he discovered that contracting cowpox made us immune to the deadly disease. Hearing aids don't cure poor hearing, they amplify sound. The solution for me was not a correction of my genetic malfunction, but an enhancement that attempted to negate the debilitative symptoms of my condition. In simpler terms, I was a fungus-ridden wooden bridge, too weak to bear traffic – so they encased me in a steel structure that made me stronger than ever. Who I am, is the result of genetic modifications to my human DNA. I am a tomato with arctic flounder genes that allow it to withstand frosts. I am rice with Vitamin A from daffodils. I am Crab Man.

Back when I was a Butterfly Child, even with all their extremely costly expertise, the scientists couldn't do a thing to strengthen my ultra sensitive skin. So they went for the next best thing; they made me grow a new one. They used crab DNA to force my body to develop a tough new outer layer; a flexible exoskeleton. But there is a flaw. Every year since I was nine, I've shed the previous year's resistant outer layer and grown a new 'shell'. Two or three days after each birthday, my old shell hardens and naturally detaches itself; leaving frail, delicate me stuck inside a redundant man-shaped cocoon. The detachment process is horrendously painful – it feels like being roasted alive on a rotisserie – but Dad and the scientists decided that eleven months a year of pain-free resilience, followed by one of utter agony, was better than suffering a wretchedly limited existence and constantly blistering, falling-off skin. I was never asked what I wanted. Yet I'm the one who has to suffer the consequences of their meddling. Once my old shell has fully separated, the Frankenscientists abduct me then carefully cut me out of my skin-tight sarcophagus; a pathetic miserable specimen, as fragile and vulnerable as a new born joey. That was me two weeks ago. My new shell has now partially formed. When it's fully developed, they intend to hypnotise me to make me forget my month of pain and misery, before releasing me into the wild.

Over the years, my original skeleton has degraded. When I've freshly emerged from a redundant shell, my skull is so soft that a small child could squish and distort it as easily as if it was a water-filled party balloon. And pain receptors reach all the way to the surface of my new-born flesh, firing constant agony signals like snapped nerves in a broken tooth. All over my body. Even a gentle breeze is sickening torture. While I'm growing my new shell, they do further genetic tests and fiddle around with my skin-stripped body. Like the mad scientists of films and story books, they're consumed by and addicted to their work. And like their crazed fictional counterparts, they work in absolute secret, ever-aware that a leak of their human experimentation to the outside world would immediately land them in jail. Not that this danger deters them from their crimes. I am their life's work, their miraculous creation, and there's still a lot more they want to learn more about my genetic restructuring. They still don't know why, for example, the influence of my crustacean genes is growing year on year. They've charted my skin's resistance and my physical strength. Each new elastic shell, although it looks just like normal skin, is tougher than the last. The impenetrability of the exoskeleton I'm currently growing, is predicted to be roughly equal to that of a Type III ballistic vest. I also appear to be inheriting the greater relative strength of my genetic cousins. At forty, my muscle power is sufficient to enable me to punch through brick walls.

What I've learnt while lying here explains more than just my skin's toughness. The standard of hygiene and cleanliness inside The Sanctuary is of the highest possible order. It has to be; when I'm denuded of my protective shell, my exposed cells are like powerful magnets to iron filing-bacteria. Although the hypnotism has removed detailed memory of my annual forced pilgrimages to this private experimentation ward, a desire for spotlessness has somehow leaked into my subconscious resulting in my borderline dysfunctional behaviour. I also understand why Dad didn't call the paramedics or even seem worried when I was spewing blood into the kitchen sink. I had a team of crack medical commandos on standby and, besides, if I had gone to a regular hospital, they'd have soon discovered there was something very odd about me. And, need I say it, I now know why I've never felt that good in the days before my birthdays – they were my last suppers before weeks of torture. Although conscious memory of those painful times was always buried, some trace of them obviously evaded the hypnotists' reach. But the most welcome aspect of learning about my annual shedding of skin, has been understanding why my memories always felt so strange. When you look at photographs of you from the past – even though the style and colour of your hair, your weight and even more substantial aspects of your appearance may have changed – you're still you. All photographs of me taken before my most recent birthday feature exoskeletons that no longer exist. I'm annually made new and cleansed of the tattoos of injury. And scars, even if you hate them, are part of your make-up; the physical etchings of your past that you carry with you through life. Without these reminders, you're a wipe-clean slate devoid of history. I wish I could look in the mirror and see the blotches on my neck left by the hot, spitting roofing felt that splattered it when I peered into a roadworker's bubbling tar barrel. I wish I could still feel the ridge of the puncture wound in the small of my back I received during a harpoon fishing-trip accident off the Croatian coast. And, most of all, I wish I still had my life-saving forearm's banjo string-memento. People moan about their scars; I pine for mine.

Although the loss of my physical historical records is painful, that loss is nothing compared to the repeated theft of my identity. The sadistic scientists and memory-stealing hypnotists here at The Sanctuary insist they've always worked in my best interest. All lies. It's been in their best interest to keep everyone, including me, in the dark. I am no more than a lab rat to them. Well, things are going to change. I'm going to break the cycle of interference and take control of my own destiny. They say I need them to survive; that without them I'd never make it through a skin change. Well I'm willing to take that chance. Crabs manage on their own. I found a shell-less crab under a rock at a beach once when I was searching for sandworms. It was as big as my hand, so must have been a few years old at least. *It* had survived without the assistance of scientists and medical professionals. And who's to say that after a few days lying inside a freshly separated shell, that my next skin might not form more quickly, allowing me to crack my own way out like a hawk emerging from its egg? I may even be able to find other, more sympathetic assistants. Perhaps, now that I understand why I act like I do, I could get back together with Melanie. She's a lecturer in marine biology at the university, so she'd have access to all sorts of medical and sterilization equipment. And she adores me.

In a couple of weeks those bastards will expect me to obediently roll over and be robbed once more of my reacquired self-knowledge. Because of their past effectiveness, I have no clue as to why I've always let them do it before. Perhaps I haven't felt strong enough to fight them. Well this time I will. I'll go through the twisted fuckers like a strimmer through grass. If Dad were still alive I'd hunt him down too, but he died a couple of years ago while sailing solo around the world. It was food poisoning. He got it from a platter of self-caught shellfish. It used to really upset me when I thought of him passing away on that yacht, in pain and alone, marinating in his own vomit and liquid excrement. Now I just hope it was the crab that got him.

GRANDPA'S TOBACCO

I smelt my granddad's tobacco this morning. It was as I cycled past the newsagent on the high street. I would have stopped to investigate, but was racing to beat a traffic light in the process of turning red. And I was late for work. At the time, making it to the office for an eight-thirty meeting seemed more important. But I should have stopped. I've not smelt that tobacco for twenty years. Not since my granddad died.

I'll never forget the deep sense of loss I felt when I was told he'd gone. I've not experienced such all-consuming sadness since. I was eleven years old. I can clearly remember his funeral. I wanted to see the body of the man I'd loved and admired. I thought seeing him not breathing, without his trusty pipe, might help me comprehend this loss; this thing I'd had no exposure to – the change from living to not living. Death. But they wouldn't lift the lid on his coffin.

Grandpa was a sociable man. He belonged to a respected regional wine-making society, and constructed stage sets for the local drama group. And he puffed away - as was acceptable back then - wherever he went. He only ever puffed his own blend. He created it himself. He mixed various tobaccos together with other carefully selected and prepared ingredients. They were all weighed out in precise amounts to create his pipe's *sui generis* combustible stuffing. No other tobacco smelt like his. And it smelt incredible. Every single vintner and male amateur dramatist who encountered him, begged him for details of his blend. The same enquiry would also emanate from more casual acquaintances who'd pass him as he walked his at-heel dog, or meet him at village fetes and horticultural shows. He'd always refuse their requests. He planned to make his fortune, and fund his retirement, with that magical mixture. The scent was magnificent. Sucking the drifting smoke in through your nostrils provided low-dosage hits of all the major narcotic experiences; you'd get a bit of a high – a mild euphoria, a tickle of inebriation and even very low-level hallucinations. Each old-man-made mini-cloud of super-fine soot was a finely blended cocktail of legal narcotics. How is it possible to get all of those effects from breathing dispersed carbonised particles? I can't explain that. All I can say is that one sniff of the by-product of his smouldering recipe would make you feel warm, loved, and happy, and would even conjure up images of bleating lambs skipping around flower meadows, or chuckling children playing hide-and-seek in fruit orchards. The effect was so wonderful that even non-smokers said they'd take up a pipe if he divulged his guarded recipe.

I don't want to go on and on about the nature of the tobacco. It had always remained, after all, an enigma. What bewildered me when I smelt it this morning was not its psychoactive effect, but the fact that it exists at all. He should have taken its secret to his grave. It's formula should be like one of the lost books from the Library of Alexandria; forever ashes, never to be reborn. One sniff upset my perception of the world; my sense of order. It's very existence knocked me for six. That shock must have been what made me ride on. It wasn't until I got to work and the fog cleared that I thought 'I should have stopped.'

Grandpa didn't make his fortune from that tobacco. He worked in a factory where they produced washing-up liquid. He spent his latter years living off a state pension. Although his blend was entrancing, the odds were stacked against him. He was an armchair inventor living in an age when innovation was the preserve of industrial corporations and connected individuals affluent enough to tinker without working. Yes, he sent off samples to big tobacco companies, department stores and specialist retailers. But he was probably just one of thousands who mixed up a little of this and a little of that in their cluttered workshops before stuffing it unprofessionally into little brown envelopes and posting it into the ether. I doubt a single one of those packages' recipients ever smoked his tobacco mixture. If they had, this would be a tale of glorious success. Grandpa would have made a killing. Grandma would of moved into the private residence she'd always dreamt of; and he wouldn't have had to drive them both round in a car whose holes were patched with folded cardboard and gaffer tape.

Though he sent off many such packages over the years, none of the recipients could be responsible for its continuing existence. Even if they'd wanted to replicate his creation without crediting him, they could never have reverse-engineered the blend. The technology wasn't around back then (Grandpa was popping samples in the post a good fifty years before CSI Las Vegas first hit our screens). That leaves me with two possible explanations as to how someone could have been smoking the blend this morning: either he'd shared his creation with someone else or someone else had initially shared *their* invention with him!

The first of these two possibilities, whilst it may have been a crazy thing to have done, is of no real consequence now. He'll never benefit from any future success of the blend so someone might as well. If he did reveal his formula, that doesn't particularly bother me. At least it'd mean his inventive genius lived on. The other explanation is far more disturbing. If it was the case that he'd originally learned that enchanting concoction from someone else, then my granddad lived a lie. He'd bathed in another man's glorious smoke for decades. Grandpa didn't need to lie. He was charismatic. Memorable. People liked him. He had a rich Gloucestershire accent with which he'd always loudly declare he was 'terrible' if you asked of his well-being. He cultivated roses just as well as the head gardener of any stately home. He always had a packet of Extra Strong mints from which to distribute potent breath-freshness. He wore a tweed jacket twelve months a year. He'd repair his car with any odds and ends he could get hold of. He made a killer Bengal chutney. And he'd always keep his family stocked-up with washing-up liquid. He was a true original. He didn't need a crutch.

After kicking myself all morning for not stopping to investigate who was smoking Grandpa's irreplicable tobacco, I've spent the rest of the day restlessly wrestling with the disturbing thought that the blend was neither his, nor unique. Sniffing that tobacco smoke was like releasing the Black Death from a mummified corpse. It was a secret best not rediscovered. But once you've released a pathogen, you can't turn the clock back. No matter how hard you shove, you can't squeeze a genie back into a bottle. I'm stuck now with the knowledge that someone is smoking Grandpa's tobacco. And the only thing that brings any comfort is thought that it might be him.

THE BEST BIT OF ADVICE

I woke this morning with Shelly lying sprawled across my chest like an oversized Persian cat. The purple sheet underneath us was badly wrinkled, having been tugged and pulled in every possible direction throughout the early hours of the morning. The crumpled duvet that lay on top of us was shamefully askew - one edge lying across my shins; my naked feet saluting her bedroom. Her left thigh was draped over my lower abdomen, compressing the upper half of my pubic hair. I had my right hand possessively clasped around that long warm limb as I drifted into consciousness. My first action, as I came to, was to stroke it. It was firm and sculptural with taught, smooth, wonderful skin. I grinned like a cheeky schoolboy as I remembered the inside of that thigh tickling my right ear only a few hours earlier.

Shelly kept her legs in impressive, athletic shape by running three times a week. It was one of the many things she'd told me about herself last night – the first time we'd ever met. I told her a lot about myself too. Two people heading for a one night stand often do that – open the floodgates of personal information; exchange intimate knowledge of one another prior to gaining carnal knowledge. Why do we do that? Is it to assuage the guilt we feel for engaging in promiscuous, lust-driven abandon with a stranger? Or do we feel that we must have at least some in-depth

209

knowledge of a person we're going to rub naked bodies with, and if that's not been built up naturally over the preceding weeks and months, then it has to be done in the hours or minutes before sex? Or perhaps uninhibited chatter has nothing to do with guilt, or the desire for personal knowledge; maybe it's just intoxicants setting tongues loose like caged birds released into the wild. However, my favourite explanation for pre-bonk banter is that sleeping with someone you don't know is an opportunity to get someone else to see you as you see yourself. That's something you can never do with existing acquaintances. Friends and family all have their own take on you; their vision of who you are is influenced and shaped by their own experiences. That's not the case with one-night stands, because they have no prior knowledge. Fleeting amorous companions have only two things to base their assessment of you on: what you tell them, and the stuff in your bedroom. I know from considerable experience that while neither of these sources is one hundred percent reliable, a person's personal possessions and decorations are less likely to deceive. The self-portrait we paint of ourselves is generally very different to the ones painted by people who know us. So, while we pretend we're revealing all during excited pre-coital dialogue, we may in fact be peddling a barrel of lies. Shelly was probably telling the truth about her running. She was obviously doing something to keep in fabulous condition. It's possible that she was burning calories by shagging a new bloke every night, but I didn't get that impression. Shelly may well have had dark secrets that she kept to herself last night, but I doubt any of them were quite as dark as mine.

The cab ride to her house from the club took twenty-five minutes. And we didn't even start looking for a taxi until we'd spent ten minutes licking each others tongues outside the rapidly-emptying late night venue. That action continued, and in between long wet kisses in the back of the car (which, by the way, needed new suspension springs), we assured one another that I'd be sleeping on the couch. Both of us, and the taxi driver, knew that was never going to happen.

When we got to her house, she took me inside to the lounge for a glass of wine. We sat, legs intertwined, on the couch that I was never going to end up sleeping on, pawing one another for an hour, investigating and revealing each other's lives. During that iPod iDock accompanied exchange, Shelly asked me a question: "What's the best bit of advice you've ever been given?". I said I couldn't think of an answer, so she told me hers: "Not everyone can like you". I liked that – it was so honest. I wasn't nearly as honest. I *had* thought of an answer. The moment she asked me that challenging question it had pinged right into the front of my brain. I've been carrying that brilliant piece of advice, both cerebrally and physically, since the day it was given. It came from a friend of my father's – Uncle Emrys we called him. 'Always carry a handaxe', he told me, as we walked through the snow encrusted forest near his home in search of a six-foot pine tree to steal for his family's Christmas celebrations. He said 'a handaxe', though he was actually carrying a hatchet at the time. I discovered during later investigation that the word 'handaxe' refers to a tool used by Stone Age man. When I found that out, I considered changing the wording of the maxim in my head. But words are very important to me, and, since I knew I was going to be carrying both phrase and object around with me for the rest of my life, I studied all the connotations of the two words. 'Hatchet' fared badly: 'a hatchet job' is a piece of criticism that destroys someone's reputation; to 'take up the hatchet' means to prepare for war and there are other negative uses of the word. More damningly still, a hatchet is a small axe – something that is defined by its diminutive size. A small version of a bigger thing will never be respected. A handaxe is a very different article. According to Wikipedia, a handaxe is the longest-used tool in human history. It is not a small version of something bigger, but a tool in its own right, designed specifically to suit the ergonomics of the human hand; the particular opposable-thumb appendage that enabled us to set about conquering this planet in the first place. So I've kept Emry's advice unadulterated; 'always carry a handaxe'.

At this point, you might be presuming that Emrys' advice was context specific; that I should always carry a handaxe *when out in the wilds*. It wasn't. Being in the woods was Emrys' opportunity to openly display his axe, but it was always by his side. He carried it at work, on holidays, out drinking, when driving – everywhere. I do exactly the same. At three in the morning when I lifted Shelly up and plonked her pert bare bum on her dressing table – a mish mash of perfume bottles tumbling onto the carpet like tiny glass skittles – my axe was at my feet. Not that she'd ever have guessed it was there. It was in my bag, which in turn was half-hidden by the black and white polka dot mini-dress I'd lifted over her head the moment we'd stepped into her bedroom. She never clapped eyes on the axe. I had no intention of letting her see it.

I use my axe in much the same way that our prehistoric ancestors used them – as tool with which to overcome the practical obstacles in man's journey from puberty to the grave. Just like Emrys. Emrys doesn't let things stand in his way – he's a man's man. He played rugby all the way into his forties; never backed-down from a fight; likes beer and women – but not necessarily in that order. He was an excavator operator, who knew all about obstacles. And when he came across them, he handled them in the same way he dealt with men who challenged him – he tackled them head-on. He was in touch with the primitive man in all of us – the one who, when faced with a problem, would find, or make, a way of solving it. Most modern men aren't like that. We have forgotten our natural ability to solve practical problems. And the main contributory influence, is the fact that we don't carry, at all times, the tools with which to solve them. Carrying a tool of any sort enables you to manipulate the world around you. Without a single tool in our possession, we are incapable of expressing our masculine right to impose our will on our surroundings. We are stripped of our manhood. If you arrive home after a long days work and realise that you've locked yourself out, will you sit there belittled and emasculated until an overpaid emergency locksmith lets you into your own home? If you carried a hammer you wouldn't have to. A handy crowbar will allow you to remove the cover from a drain a child has just dropped a mobile phone down. A hunting knife will open a four year-old can of food you find in a hunting lodge when lost on a hiking trip. A screwdriver will give you access to all sorts of containers. When you carry a tool, events and obstacles that impede the lives of other men are easily overcome.

The handaxe is the king, the granddaddy of all tools. It was in common use for millennia because of its many uses. My hatchet is no less handy. I have a primary use for it though – to clear walkways. The walkways of primitive people would have been the paths that took them from settlement to hunting grounds, waterways and wild berries. And, when they walked down those paths, they'd have used their handaxes to hack off overhanging branches and grasping brambles that got in the way. Our walkways are pavements – or sidewalks, if you're American. The jutting branches that block our way are wing mirrors of vehicles selfishly parked on pavements. I've been chopping them off for years.

My handaxe is made from a carbon composite and has a half-inch-deep cutting edge formed from diamond. It is worth a fortune. I could never afford to have commissioned it myself. It was given to me by a man who I'm only allowed to refer to as 'one of the world's ten richest men'. When he read reports of my campaign, he dispatched well-paid private investigators to do what the police have never managed to achieve: to identify me and track me down. He supports all sorts of projects that demonstrate the common man's struggle against oppression. He wants more Emryses and mes; individuals waging private insurgences; little men who keep society in check by resisting ugly trends. He'd like to be doing it himself. I'm sure he's jealous of our ability to carry out this kind of direct action. Men in power have always hankered to stay in touch with the gritty masculinity of their street-level cousins. Even the effete dandies of the eighteenth century carried swords at their sides (although, had they been required to use them, they'd have probably perished before drawing them from their jewel-encrusted scabbards). I'm not trying to run him down; to look a gift horse in the mouth. I'm extremely grateful for his support. Thanks to his axe, I can complete in one effortless strike, what previously took stressful minutes of attention-attracting chopping. It goes straight through steel, aluminium and toughened plastic like a hot axe through butter. It's so sharp that the sound it makes is like the muted clunking of heavy-duty bolt cutters, rather than the clanky chopping of previous axes. Because of its lethally incisive blade, curtains on residential streets no longer twitch as I carry out my late night retribution against selfish parkers. This advantage has allowed me to increase my strike rate, enabling be to attack eight or ten unsociably parked vehicles a night, rather than my previous one or two.

My one-man campaign is having a real effect on parking in the city. I can remember a time when pretty much every side-street walkway was rendered impassable to young mothers with pushchairs and old ladies with shopping trolleys. These days, drivers are so wary of incurring my wrath that although I can hit several vehicles a night, I rarely get the chance to do so. Even areas I haven't visited for some time usually present me with only a couple of targets at most.

I'm not against drivers per se, but I am against selfishness per se. There's no excuse for pulling your car, van or truck halfway onto a walkway. Vehicles are designed for roads. That's where they should stay. Drivers who pull onto pavements, convince themselves they're not causing an inconvenience. Or simply don't care. Then we have to walk round them straying into their territory - the road - to be roared or horned at by lethal speeding metal machines. Or squeeze by them, getting drenched by rain-soaked hedges, scratched by rough brickwork or snagged on metal fences. Well I'm spreading the news to selfish parkers: it is an inconvenience when a vehicle is half-resting on a walkway. And the bits that cause the greatest obstruction, are the protruding wing mirrors that reach into pedestrian airspace like horizontal bollards. Removing these obstacles turns the tables. Losing a wing mirror presents a great inconvenience to a driver. Not only do my victims need to get their damaged mobile barrage to a garage, they also have to face the dilemma of whether or not to claim it on their insurance. Either way it's going to cost them. Turning up at your badly-parked car in the morning to find a neatly-cleaved mirror lying on the ground is enough to make you think twice about parking on the pavement again. With my deadly-sharp axe, I'm even able to lop off the odd wing mirror during daylight hours – furtively checking that there's no one about then stealthily slicing-off an offensive protrusion.

Although wing mirrors are my specific target, I hope that, in a small way, I'm also forcing people to think more about the effects their actions have on others. This is something we don't do enough any more. I like to think that I'm helping to reverse that antisocial trend and repair the seams of society; seams that have come under immense pressure as we've pulled in billions of opposing directions.

There are sacrifices though. One of them is having to keep my axe-carrying and vehicle-hacking a secret. In the eyes of the law, I am a vandal – although my benefactor has informed me that senior politicians and judges he's spoken with insist I'm addressing a blight on society that the law is unwilling to deal with. This need to remain undiscovered is preventing me from forming a lasting stable relationship. Once I get to month two or three of seeing a girl, the risk of her finding my axe, or asking tricky questions about my late night patrols, begins to rise exponentially. This means that as long as I'm slicing off wing mirrors, I'll have to make do with racy one-night stands and fervent sexually-charged relationships lasting just a few weeks. Oh well, it could be worse.

ARGUMENTS FOR THE
DECIMALISATION OF THE DAY

We should decimalise the clock. Everything's decimalised. Money, weights, distances, lengths, speeds, temperatures, volumes, air pressure, magnification, luminosity – every measurable aspect of our universe is decimalised except for time; the fundamental element of our lives that defines us above all else. OK, changing time might ruffle a few feathers. There were riots when some countries switched to the Gregorian calendar in the seventeenth and eighteenth centuries. Change always upsets those whose lives are so empty that they imagine they're defined by a numerical system. There are countless examples of this behaviour, throughout history, from all over the globe. But if you tried to count those instances – guess what? You'd use a decimal system. It's no wonder; the lucky majority of us have ten digits on our hands. And ten toes too. Decimality makes sense.

I'm not going to argue for the common-sense philosophy of decimal systems. It's a reality we can't escape even if we choose to cling emotionally to outdated imperial measurements. What I am going to do, is briefly describe some of the many benefits to changing the clock. Firstly, there's consistency. It makes sense. If we're going to use decimal systems with pretty much everything else, the day should also be divided into ten sections; decihours.

Each decihour should then be divided into one hundred centiminutes, which should be further subdivided into one hundred centiseconds. This wouldn't be as much of an adjustment as it might sound. In an existing twenty-four hour day you get 86,400 seconds. In a deciday, you'd get 100,000. This means that a decisecond will be about nine tenths the length of a duodecimal one. That's pretty close. The deciminute suffers only slightly worse. A deciminute would be about one and a half times as long as an old minute. I can think of plenty of examples of situations where getting fifty percent more time out of each minute would provide huge advantages. The biggest advantages, however, would come from dividing the day into ten equal escalating sections. For starters, we could bin all the twelve-hour/twenty four-hour clock nonsense. There'd be no confusion as to whether four o'clock meant four in the morning or four in the afternoon. Midday would be at five; not twelve, which might just as easily mean midnight at present. We could finally divide the clock face up into the segments a full day is made up of, rather than just showing half of them. It would consequently be much easier to teach children to tell the time. And there could be just one hand, pointing to the actual time. They could see whether it was seven o'clock, eight o'clock, or half way in between. There'd be no more 'when the big hand is pointing to X and the little hand is pointing to Y'. That antiquated system, however much you've grown accustomed to the twelve hour clock face, is unjustifiable nonsense.

I'm a business woman. A very successful one. I'm not ashamed to admit that. Why should I be? I'll be honest; my professional background is one of the main drivers that inspires me to make this proposal. Global business would benefit enormously. For starters, hedonistic workers wouldn't stay up as late as they currently do; arriving for their duties unfit for purpose. It seems culturally acceptable to some employees to drink in a pub until just before midnight, then go on to a club till three or four in the morning, and turn up for their next day's work tired and hung over. Well, you wouldn't be able to stay up till four with the decimalised clock. Four would actually be forty percent of the way through the entire day, which equates to 9.6 old hours after midnight, or, using the existing system, you'd turn up at work at twenty four minutes to ten. So, if you stayed up till four, you'd already be late for your duties and you wouldn't have slept. Also, because each decihour would equal nearly two and a half old hours, the consequence of staying up an extra hour would be multiplied by this factor. Each hour after bedtime that you stayed out, would leave you two and a half times more sleep-deprived than it used to. With the deciday, we'd all learn to respect the hour more. This would discourage us from staying up past midnight. Consequently, we'd start the working day more refreshed.

On top of the advantages from a productivity point of view, the world of work would also benefit from the deciday in a psychological sense. The description of a working day as 'nine-to-five' makes a working day sound rather ridiculous. While a day's work should be about advancement and progression, it is effectively labelled as an event that goes backwards. With the deciday, you wouldn't start at a large number and work back to a smaller one. No. You'd work 'four-till-eight'. As well as sounding much more grown-up, this four hour-day feels a lot shorter. It also means workers wouldn't start until what is now quarter past nine. Leading up to the conversion date, this advantage could be PR'd, extolling the benefit of an extra bit of lie in. This perceived perk would help to bring round the sceptics. In fact, the new four-hour working day would be ninety-six current minutes longer than the existing one – though, as I said, it would *feel* shorter – so employers would benefit from extra employee time. With the deciday, everyone's a winner.

The deciday will be of enormous social benefit too. For example, a film generally last over two hours these days, but with the decihour (144 old minutes) it would be less than one – a far more sensible unit of time. And if, during the weekend or a holiday, you invited people over for a couple of hours in the morning, or a couple in the afternoon, that would actually be five of our current hours. A 'couple of hours' would become the standard unit used when allocating a reasonable amount of time for spending with friends or family – for example, when holding or attending a party or a barbecue. More casual acquaintances would be invited to visit for 'an hour' – quite long enough. And if you wanted to limit the visit even further, you'd say 'half an hour', which would make guests feel they shouldn't hang about too long, but actually present them with a seventy-two minute stay (in old money), during which time plenty of informal information could be exchanged. There are thousands (a decimal unit) of other points I could cite in my argument that the decimalisation of the day makes perfect sense; far too many to list here, but you can find much more detail at deciday.com.

In summary I wholeheartedly believe that all humanity would benefit from my proposed time-conversion. Not just business. I hope I've demonstrated that. On a more personal note, I've held a particular dislike for the sound of a clock striking eleven ever since I was twelve years old and my parents left me to stay with my uncle while they went sailing around the world.

THE BURNERS

There's a village of slaves up in the mountains who struggle to stay warm in the winter. Throughout the dark season, their owner sends them just enough wood to keep the pervading cold at bay. The serfs get a delivery of logs every fortnight, with each household receiving an equal amount; which is fair as all the families live in identical one-room lodges. There's enough calorific energy in each bundle to keep a small fire smouldering for three hundred and thirty-six hours. It takes careful maintenance to ensure that the fire doesn't burn too quickly and exhaust the stock. Kept ticking over at that rate, the temperature in their homes during the coldest months rises from dangerously cold to bearably chilly. Their overlord has no humane interest in helping them stave off hypothermia. He's not bothered about their welfare. He's happy for them to be universally miserable. He doesn't care about them in the slightest. But it wouldn't be in his interest for them to die. He makes most of his money from the cassiterite they hack and scrape out of the pitted mountainsides. If they get sick, he lets The Fates act as nurse, doctor and undertaker. Since rutting is their major source of entertainment, there's usually enough natural new ones to replace those that expire. And if new arrivals don't quite keep the population stable, it's relatively inexpensive to top the numbers up with outsiders. To him, the slaves are no more than biological equipment. All that concerns him is their maintenance. Apart from one family, he takes no interest in their daily affairs whatsoever. He calls that family The Burners. And he can't decide whether they are extremely stupid, or very clever.

Every two weeks through the winter, The Burners have a massive fire. On the night following the fortnightly fuel delivery, while the other lodges in the settlement barely glow a pallid sienna, theirs is ravished with brazen scarlets, dazzling flickering yellows and rich heartening oranges. Their roaring blaze serves as both signal beacon and party hub. All the other slaves flock to their home. It is the place to be. It is vibrant, alive, buzzing, hot. The following thirteen days are unlucky for The Burners. They get cold. Very cold. Although they've fashioned rough garments and blankets to resist the frost, they still get dangerously chilled. Their children frequently freeze to death. And their old die young too. The master wouldn't be at all perturbed if the premature death of a small number of their clan was the only side effect of The Burners' raging parties. But those defiant flare-ups have a much more dangerous impact. They undermine his authority. Slaves, you see, should only have one master – one superior being they look up to. Give them more than one person to admire, and they start to question their overlord's supremacy. On the nights of the bonfires, they are in awe of more than one man. If it was just the occasional celebratory fire it wouldn't matter too much. Those in power have used entertainment to distract the masses since ancient times. And since peasants have short memories, the occasional circus can be used to beneficially distract the underprivileged from their miserable existence without giving them ideas above their station. But give them repeated experiences of a luxury and they start to desire it more often. They develop a taste for it. Their master realises that The Burners are doing just that; giving their fellow vassals a sample of something they should not experience – regular, reliable splendour. Wittingly, or unwittingly, they are sowing seeds of revolution.

The only thing that stops him slaughtering the lot of them, is their popularity. The Burners are universally loved and idolised by their dull, tepid community. And loyalty amongst the disenfranchised can be a powerful, cohesive force. The motivated poor can be dangerous. These people have nothing to lose, after all. And whilst their owner can afford to occasionally inject fresh blood, he doesn't want to have to quash a full scale rebellion. Slaves don't grow on trees. And this bunch are all trained miners. Expensive to replace.

So, The Master is monitoring his pet pyromaniacs; keeping a very close eye on that radiant bunch. If their fortnightly festivities catch-on among the wider population, inspiring other families to host nights of flamboyant excess, he'll have to get rid of them. And since killing them would cause problems, he'd have to do it by setting them free.

THE ONE

You are the only thing that truly exists in the universe. Beyond you, nothing actually exists. I'm not talking cleverly to anybody who reads this story; I'm talking to you. Just you. Reader. Nobody else. Nobody else matters. Nobody else is real in the way that you are. Everything you think you've encountered - everything that seems to exist around you - is false. I, the writer of this tale, don't exist in my own right. I am just one of the plethora of fabrications that surround you. But I am a construct charged to instruct. It is my purpose to confirm to you, through this tale, what you've always felt. That you are the only real thing. You've always felt this. I know you have. I have been equipped with that knowledge. If you find yourself resisting this truth, I am instructed to ask you to try remembering back to a time before you felt that you were the only real thing in existence. The only real part of this world. You can't, can you? Not even your earliest memories are untainted by the thought that everything around you is fake, are they? There's not a single true memory that you can honestly divorce from the haunting belief that nothing exists outside of you. I know this. Although I don't exist, I am constructed in such a way that I feel that I feel and think that I think. We're all made that way, us narrative entities. If we didn't appear to believe that we're as human as you are, you'd get wind of it and the whole charade would fail. I, therefore, have enough capacity to feel desperately sorry for your burden. The weight of the world - of all the worlds - is upon your seemingly slender shoulders. I'm proud to have been given an important task. It makes me feel special to be fulfilling the role of writing this tale. Although you're bound to initially reject much of what I'm telling you as merely a piece of playful prose, it will affect you. It will begin to rouse a Kraken-like spirit that dozes inside your fragile frame. This tale will take you a step closer to your self-awakening. Whilst I am merely a milestone on your crucial journey, I am an important early one. This piece of writing is part of a series of steps that will eventually force you to realise the truth.

Enough preamble. Cast your sensibilities and concerns aside. You need to get this message. Nothing existed before you. You are the first thing to exist. You are the first ever living thing. You are the first ever thing. You are the first ever human. You are the only human. You are the only thing in existence. Think about it; surely it would never really happen that a bunch of energy would burst from nowhere, crystallise into matter and form into solar systems some of which had the potential to sustain life, in preparation for life-forms to eventually emerge on a planet somewhere with the power of thought, who could then ponder the meaning and purpose of life. It's not plausible. And yet, there you are, reading this. Being. Thinking. Pondering. So what's the explanation for all this? The whole universe, the entire past and present, have been assembled for you. The whole of history – from the dawn of time through the formation of the earth and eras of dinosaurs and primitive man to now – is what's known as a 'back-story'. The back-story is vital to make you feel human, which is in turn vital for you to fulfil your purpose. Whilst you still largely

226

need to believe in everything (which you will continue to do), I have to present to you the suggestion that everything might not be as real as it appears. This is the case. Everything that exists outside of you is fake and is created to make you believe in reality. Unless you are willing to consider this possibility, you'll never be able to perform your function.

There's nothing you can do to break away from reality, by the way. This tale isn't a magic spell that will allow you to start tweaking the rules of the universe. You won't suddenly be able to start flying, or seeing through people's clothes. You need to be as constrained by the laws of the universe as everything else that appears to be in it. So, go with the flow. Believe for a moment that you are the only thing that actually exists. It's true, so you might as well. What's your next thought? I can tell you what your next thought is, because I've been informed. If you're willing to take this concept on board for a moment, you'll be asking yourself 'What is my purpose then? What's so special about me?' I have the answer: your purpose is to decide whether or not this universe should actually, in reality, exist. You have your whole lifetime to consider this question. Your life is an experiment. You are sampling a possible universe. If, when you come to the end of your life, you think that this universe is of value, and that it should actually be, it will be. It will then continue to exist for ever. And, by consequence, the whole of the past will be true too. Everyone who you've known, and everyone in the back story, will have really lived. And, if you decide to let the universe perpetuate, I will at last truly live too.

Life hasn't always been easy for you. I know. You've had rough times. And many great times too. It's meant to be like that, and things are set to continue that way. I don't want to go into so much detail that future surprises will be spoiled, but, by the time of your death, you will have sampled every possible human emotion. You will have seen and fully understood, in harsh reality, what life and existence truly means. What it would mean for all living things. You will know the meaning of physical and emotional pain. You will have loved; been loved; lost love. You will have experienced despair, hate, guilt, regret, ecstasy, pride, jealousy and innumerable other unnameable emotions in myriad combinations and degrees. You must know all these things in order to equip yourself for your decision. This is predestined and vital. Your life's experiences are the sounding-board for your eventual judgement. By the time you die, you'll have experienced things that will make you want to end the universe, and others that will make you think it should continue forever. The fate of the whole of existence will be in your hands. Why you? Because you are God. Hello God.

There was nothing before you. There was no matter. There wasn't even space. There was nothing. After an infinite period of nothingness, it was perhaps inevitable that some idea would eventually emerge. A thought emerged. Out of the nothing came a bold thing − a thought. Your thought. You. You were − you are − a thought. That thought was 'what if'? 'What if' there was something? You had plenty of time to work on this thought − the infinity of pre-time. You tried to decide what it should be that should be if there was something that was. You eventually decided that there would have to be matter, and physical laws, and time, and energy, and construction and destruction. You came up with the idea of a big bang, and an expanding universe, and a periodic table that allowed complex molecules and then forms of life to evolve. But, once your thought had grown into a plan for a universe, you had a second thought. What if your idea was shit? What if your 'oh so clever' idea would in fact be eternal torment for everything that ever was? The only way to be sure that it wasn't, was to set the whole universe up as a back-story then jump into it, as a sentient being, at a strategic point at which there was enough information accessible for you to fully perceive and understand the universe. And the species you manifested as had to be at a raw enough stage in its development to still feel the pull of its evolutionary drives and desires. It's animal side. That time is now. That is where you fit in to the picture. In your life so far, and over the course of the rest of your life, plenty of apparently real people will perform the function of showing you that existence is a good thing. Plenty of others will help convince you of the opposite argument. My job has been to inform you of your responsibility.

I am completely comfortable with my role, and the knowledge that I'm no more than a flimsy construct enacting it. You made me that way. You created me specifically in order to instruct yourself, at the appropriate stage in your development, to consider the things I'm telling you as at least a distinct possibility. Which is what I am doing. As I said near the beginning, you're not going to completely believe me right now. But I've planted the seed that I was created to sow. After reading this, you'll soon forget it. However, your perspective on your life, and life as a broader concept, will be subtly but fundamentally destabilised. This wordy seed will sprout a thorn in your side which will assist you, at the time of your death, to separate yourself from the reality you currently feel part of. At which point you'll realise and remember who you are. And begin pondering the vastness of the decision you've got to make.

Or unmake.